★

He watched from a secluded corner as Hannah's body, covered by a white sheet, was quietly wheeled down the hall and out the back door. It had been so simple—a pillow over her face for a few minutes. Of course, he'd been cautious. He'd waited until the middle of the night and made sure the RN and one aide on duty were in the skilled-nursing end of the hall. He'd known they would be busy there for some time. Earlier in the day, he had scouted out the room and had been pleased to see her name on the bed nearest the door. Perfect.

He'd kept thinking about this Hannah throughout the afternoon, and then it dawned on him who she was. She'd been in that group from the junior college. The group that had turned against him. Well, she'd paid for it now. There was only one more left who had tormented him back then. And that one would soon pay also.

★

MURDER in EDEN

Helen Goodman

WORLDWIDE®

TORONTO • NEW YORK • LONDON
AMSTERDAM • PARIS • SYDNEY • HAMBURG
STOCKHOLM • ATHENS • TOKYO • MILAN
MADRID • WARSAW • BUDAPEST • AUCKLAND

To Emma and Patty, my constant cheerleaders.

MURDER IN EDEN

A Worldwide Mystery/September 2007

First published by Hilliard & Harris.

ISBN-13: 978-0-373-26613-5
ISBN-10:   0-373-26613-8

Acknowledgment

I wish to thank the members of my critique group for their invaluable help and their encouragement: Nancy Gates, Wendy Greene, Diane Berry, Dorothy O'Neill, Betty DiMeo, Ellen Hunter and Pam Blackwood.

ONE

THE BUTTERFLIES WERE coming closer and closer. Teasing her. Taunting her. They knew she was trapped just as they were. She felt a sudden empathy with prisoners. But instead of bars and barbed wire imprisoning her, it was a wheelchair, and a nursing home with yellow butterfly wallpaper.

Fonnie Beachum was jolted out of her pity-party by a tremulous voice.

"Evil. He's evil." Fonnie heard the disturbing words before she saw the speaker. "Evil. He hurts people." Hannah, her face fearful, her bony hands shaking, scuffled up behind Fonnie's wheelchair. She squeezed into the corner rocker and started lurching wildly. Her words came in disconnected gasps. "He hurts people. He wants to hurt me."

Hannah's agitation perplexed Fonnie. It was most unusual for her. Fonnie once described her old friend and now roommate as pleasantly demented. Hannah was often disoriented, but not often disturbed. She would smile, talk nonsense, go on her merry way. But now she was agitated, deeply troubled about something.

Fonnie reached over with her right hand, slowed the

rocker, patted her roommate's arm. "It's all right. Now just calm down and tell me about it. What happened to upset you?" Fonnie's voice was soft and even, modulated to reassure the anxious, the panicky, the fearful—a tone she'd perfected during her forty years as a nurse. It seldom failed.

Hannah braked to a stop, uncurled her arms, and grasped Fonnie's proffered hand. "I saw him." Hannah sucked in a gob of air and let it slither out. "I'm sure it was him."

"Who? Who did you see?" Fonnie allowed no sign of irritation in her voice. She knew she had to be patient to get a straight story from her rattled friend.

"Deacon. I saw Deacon. He's here." Hannah dropped Fonnie's hand, brushed strands of stringy gray hair from her eyes, cowered back in her chair. "He's evil." Hannah's thin shoulders shuddered and she clutched the arms of the rocking chair. The veins on the backs of her shriveled hands stood out like highways on a road map. "He used to be so pretty and seemed like such a nice boy, but he did bad things." Hannah gasped for breath. The long sentence strained her ailing lungs.

Again Fonnie reached over with her good hand and gave Hannah a comforting pat. "You saw someone you used to know?"

"Yes." Hannah paused. "At least I think so." Hannah's eyebrows scrunched down in a questioning gaze. "It looked like his hands. I'm sure I saw his hands."

"Hands?"

Hannah didn't answer. Her eyes took on that far-away look people get when they're trying to recall something from the distant past. The look that pleads with their thoughts, *Come back. Don't tease me. Don't float away. I need to remember.*

"Sometimes names don't match," she finally said. "His real name didn't fit." She grimaced as the memory apparently slid into place. "We nicknamed him 'Deacon,' but that didn't fit, either."

"Where did you see him? Here in the day room?"

Hannah nodded her head. "I think so. I think I saw him, and I remember the bad things. It was so long ago, but I remember."

"A deacon that does bad things?"

Hannah's eyes retreated again, her expression wary. "His God was always mad." Her voice dropped to a whisper. "Those hands…. He said they were God's hands."

"I don't understand," Fonnie said.

Hannah crawled out of the rocker, her gaze roamed the lounge, her breaths came in short pants. "I'm going to my room. He can't hurt me there."

Fonnie watched as her roommate retreated down the hall. She tried to dismiss Hannah's tale of an evil man, a deacon who did bad things as wild imaginings of a mind that had lost its moorings. The truth was, Fonnie was feeling so sorry for herself she couldn't muster up much interest in Hannah's imaginary villain.

Yesterday Amy had tried to convince Fonnie that her stay at Springwillow was only temporary. "Just until you make a little more progress with your physical therapy, Mom."

But Fonnie feared there would be no more progress. She'd spent a month in one of the best rehab units in North Carolina. If they couldn't bring her left side back to life, then probably no one could.

She wondered how long it would take for her to accept Springwillow as her home. The first thing she needed was to make some friends—friends whose brains weren't half-scrambled.

Fonnie scanned the room for people who could possibly carry on a decent conversation. She quickly eliminated Gwendolyn, huddled in front of the TV. The woman had squeezed her voluminous bulk into a morris chair, and her flabby arms waved and flapped along with the action on the screen. Fonnie assumed Gwendolyn was a very nice lady, but decided they wouldn't have much in common.

On the floral couch across the room sat a wisp of a woman, pale, petite, wearing a simple housedress. She crooned softly to her baby doll, held it against her chest, patted its back to force a burp. Fonnie had heard the aides call her Tillie. She smiled at Tillie, and almost envied her for having escaped through the time barrier. But Fonnie really had no desire to discuss infant care with the ancient young mother.

Lucas Parker could possibly be a candidate for conversation. He'd been briefly introduced the day before. He seemed shy, but she noticed he was holding a

National Geographic as if he were really reading it and not just drooling over the pictures, so maybe he was aware of the world around him. He appeared to have burrowed deep into the sofa pillows as if trying to disappear in their depths. His ankles were crossed and his legs were jiggling—resembling a shy schoolboy afraid to tell the teacher he has to pee. He lowered the magazine for a moment and looked her way. She saw his slightly protruding Adam's apple, his neatly trimmed mustache, his eyes peering over the wire glasses perched midway on his nose. She smiled. He quickly dove back inside the yellow magazine. Fonnie shrugged.

She continued her survey of the day room. During her orientation she'd been told that most of the alert residents liked to sit out here during the day, unless they were working on something in the craft room. Since Fonnie had never been into crafts, she concluded that the day room was indeed the best place to look for friends.

Coming toward her now was a man using a front-wheeled walker. She'd seen him earlier, but hadn't caught his name. He maneuvered his walker with the skill of a skater, skimming across the floor with grace and ease. She wondered why he had to use a walker. His extremities were all intact and moved with precision. She hoped that his mind was intact, as well.

For a moment, Fonnie felt ashamed of herself. She was analyzing her fellow residents like specimens under a microscope, hoping to find one to meet her specifications. But, my God, she reminded herself, this is a matter of self-preservation. I must find someone I can talk to.

Her scrutiny of the room was interrupted by loud voices in front of the nurses' station.

She glanced that way and saw Jean, the director of nursing, trying to reason with an irate resident. The bright fluorescent light above where the nurses worked on their charts was in sharp contrast to the dimmer lamps scattered around the day room. Now that bright light focused on two people having a rather loud discussion.

Fonnie had noticed the man before—at least she'd noticed his bald pate. It looked to Fonnie as if his hair had slipped down from the top of his head and landed just above his ears. It left him with a glabrous scalp above and a fringe of anemic fuzz below. His frontal view wasn't much better. His eyebrows and lashes were so sparse that they appeared to have retreated into his face and left his dark eyes squinting out like windows from a roofless house. Fonnie soon realized, though, that his mouth more than made up for any other deficiency he may have.

The bald head bellowed, "I've never lived with cats in my life and I'm not going to start now!" He jerked on one red suspender and stuffed his other hand in his jeans' pocket.

Both Fonnie and the walker man turned their complete attention to the battle scene.

"Mr. Jowoski," Jean said, "I assure you the cats will not bother you. We're only getting two cats to begin with and they will only be allowed in the residents' rooms who want them."

"Oh, I suppose these cats will be able to read and you'll post a sign at my door to tell them not to enter or mean old Jowoski will make cat sausage out of them. And have you ever got a whiff of cat pee? It's worse than when Tillie wets her pants."

"The cats are litter-box trained. And they will soon learn who wants their company and who doesn't."

"Well, I certainly don't. I guess I'll have to get a water pistol and shoot at them every time they come around." Fonnie detected a slight smile on the man's face as he seemed to enjoy the thought. "Whose bright idea was it anyway to convert Springwillow into an animal shelter?"

"We explained all that at the resident meeting, which you, by the way, failed to attend. It's called the Eden Alternative. The plan is to introduce plants and animals to make our facility more homelike, to reconnect our residents to nature. Most of them think it's a grand idea. It will be a way to relieve loneliness and boredom, to enhance life, to nurture the human spirit."

"Hmph! It'd take more than plants and animals to turn this place into a Garden of Eden. What other critters are you going to bring in after the cats?" The man lowered his voice some and it seemed to Fonnie that he was simmering down a little.

Jean smiled. "Birds. Of course, they'll be enclosed in an aviary. Don't you think it would be enjoyable to watch finches and parakeets flitting around?"

"Hmph! Locked up just like we are? Oh, sure, that'll be great fun."

The nurse ignored his sarcasm. "And later on we may bring in some dogs, and maybe even some rabbits—not to stay, mind you, just to visit with the residents. And of course, there's the children."

"Children? What children?"

"We're making arrangements with the preschool down the road to bring their children in from time to time to visit. Many of our residents don't get to see their grandchildren or great-grandchildren very often. They'll enjoy seeing the youngsters. And it will be a good experience for the children also—to relate to an older generation. Don't you agree?"

"Well, the kids might be all right, as long as they don't get in my way. But I don't want any animals around me."

"I assure you, Mr. Jowoski, we won't let them intrude on your space. We take your complaints very seriously."

"Well, I hope you took my complaint about the afternoon medicine nurse seriously. She was late with my four o'clock Zoloft yesterday. I need that med to make it through the day and that pissant of a nurse made me wait because she and her boyfriend were in the linen closet messing around."

Jean's smile vanished and her voice held a noticeable chill. "You know the nurse has a thirty-minute leeway to pass out the medications. Just because your med is ordered for four o'clock doesn't mean you'll get it exactly at four."

"Well, if it's late again, I'll write up a grievance."

"Good. You do that." Jean attempted another smile. "Now let's get back to the matter at hand. Just give us a chance, Mr. Jowoski. I assure you the Edenization of our facility will not affect you."

"Hmph!"

Jean gave him a tolerant grin and went on down the hall to her office. Mr. Jowoski strutted over to a dark green batwing chair and flopped down.

Fonnie was amused by the encounter. Here was a person who could talk and was not afraid to express an opinion. Not that she agreed with him, but it would be interesting to get to know him. She was familiar with people like Mr. Jowoski. They regularly blew off more steam than a threatening volcano, then when they had scared everyone around, they sputtered out.

She scooted her wheelchair over to where he sat. It was slow going. She'd vetoed her daughter's suggestion to purchase a motorized chair. At that time she was still in her conqueror mode, determined to regain her lost mobility. Now she wasn't so sure.

She came up to Mr. Jowoski with a smile. "You know, one reason I chose this home was because I'd heard they were going to Edenize. I had a cat for years. Her name was Isabel. And my husband always had a dog. I miss not having animals around. I'm sorry you seem so set against it."

Mr. Jowoski looked startled, then grinned, as if grateful for a chance to continue his tirade. "Well, for starts, the name is ridiculous. They might better have named it, 'The Nature Alternative' or 'Cats are Us'."

Fonnie laughed. "Or 'Back to the Jungle'. I just saw a truck drive up with potted plants. They have ferns, rubber tree plants, cacti, and what looked like a corn plant tree."

"I noticed them, too," a soft, cultured voice put in. Fonnie looked up at the owner of the wheelie-walker. "Don't mean to intrude. But I've been wanting to meet you. Calvin Flynt here. Welcome to Springwillow."

"Thank you. I'm Fonnie Beachum." She turned away momentarily from Mr. Jowoski. "I've wanted to meet you also. And I think the greenery will be an added pleasure. Don't you?"

"I certainly do. It'll make this room more like a hotel lobby. That way, we can pretend we're visiting a few days in Atlanta or Raleigh or perhaps even Savannah."

Fonnie liked the way the names of the cities rolled off his tongue. It was like he was speaking of familiar haunts. Maybe they could compare travel memories. She loved to talk about her vacations in Hilton Head and in Asheville.

She studied his face—probably handsome in his youth—now filled with what one would call character. He still had a full head of hair, not exactly silver, more the color of an early morning frost. His soft blue eyes gazed through gold-framed glasses. A smile started with his eyes, and traveled slowly to the rest of his face. Yes, here was one of the friends she'd been looking for.

Fonnie was about to dive into what she hoped would be a stimulating conversation with him, but was disappointed when he whirled his walker around.

"We'll have to talk later. I've reserved a computer for this hour. But I'm looking forward to getting acquainted." He bobbed his head to both of them and careened off down the hall. Fonnie nodded and watched him slide away.

She nearly forgot about the man on her other side until he boomed, "You didn't ask me what *I* thought about the trees coming in."

Here was a man who liked the spotlight, Fonnie thought. She again turned her attention to him. "And what *do* you think about them?"

"I think they're great. If there are enough of them, maybe we'll get a chance to run naked through the forest."

Fonnie shuddered. "I certainly hope not. The last things I want to see are floppy boobs, bulging bellies, and listless appendages—all too tired to fight against gravity."

"Oh-o-o-!" Mr. Jowoski jerked his head. "That doesn't sound like something a sweet old lady like you should say."

"In my opinion, the smartest thing Adam and Eve ever did, was to put clothes on." She gave him a saccharine smile. "And what makes you think I'm a sweet old lady?"

"Those braids wrapped around your head. They look straight out of the nineteenth century—back when a woman knew her place and a vulgar word never crossed her lips."

Fonnie stroked the faded gray braids that started at

the back of her head and made their way in opposite directions up and across the top. Her braids, once as thick as rodeo ropes, had thinned until now her pink scalp peeped out like the setting sun through cirrus clouds. Lately she'd added extra bobbie pins to the top of her head to keep the braids from sliding down.

"Actually, I've worn these braids all my adult life because they were practical, they were easy to fix, and they kept my hair out of the way."

"And, unless I miss my guess, you also wore them because your man liked to run his hands through your long hair when you were in bed."

Mr. Jowoski's remark evoked sweet and pleasurable memories in Fonnie. Harrison used to slip off the rubber bands, untwist the braids and tangle his fingers through her locks. She nodded. "That, too." She gave a long sigh. "But I've decided, when the beautician comes tomorrow, to have my hair cut and permed. You see, I can't braid it myself any longer and the aides don't have time to help me with it."

"They don't have time for much of anything. I hear their excuses constantly." His voice rose to a falsetto. "I don't have time to get you another cup of coffee, Mr. Jowoski. I don't have time to clean your razor. It doesn't matter what I ask, they don't have time."

"Well, they don't. Nurse's aides, or Certified Nurse Assistants, as we're supposed to call them now, are overworked and under paid—and under appreciated. They do the best they can."

"And so just because they don't have time to comb your hair, you're going to have it cut. Hmph."

"That's not the only reason. Amy, that's my daughter, keeps telling me that I have to get on with my life. So I'm getting on. It's time to let go."

LET GO. It was a phrase she'd heard often in her life, a phrase she hated. She recalled one occasion. She was a young nurse, just starting work in the delivery room of the small local hospital—before high tech equipment, before neonatal ICUs. Babies born then either made it on their own or they didn't make it at all.

Fonnie closed her eyes and again saw that tiny premature baby. It was a boy. His bluish skin shimmered. Dark blood dribbled from the cut umbilical cord onto his puny legs. The doctor placed the baby in the crib and turned his attention back to the mother. "Too small," was his only comment.

But Fonnie saw the tiny breast heave upward—once, twice. "He's breathing. Maybe we can save him." Fonnie held the oxygen mask a few inches from the baby's face and watched for more movement. There was none. She placed two fingers on the infant's chest and gave a gentle push—and another—and another.

The doctor glanced over to her. "What are you doing?"

She continued the light pressure without looking up. "This baby wants to live. I can tell. He's a fighter."

The doctor shoved his stool back, slipped off his gloves, and nodded to the anaesthetist to let the mother wake up.

He crossed over to the crib, studied the small bit of humanity, reached out and took Fonnie's hands in his. "You're the one who's the fighter. But it's time to let go."

Ten years ago it was Amy who mouthed the words. Fonnie was holding Harrison's hand, watching the monster respirator inflate her husband's lungs—up, down, up, down. The muffled sound pounded against her ears, and the peaks and dips on the monitor screen did a crazy dance in front of her eyes. The body that she loved was disfigured with tubes and tape. His hands were cold and blue, but she kept squeezing them, willing life to come back. Then at some point Amy pulled Fonnie to her feet.

"Come on, Mom. It's time to let go."

But Amy wouldn't say the words when Fonnie had her stroke. Instead her daughter kept saying things like, "You can't give up, Mom. You've got to keep fighting."

So she had fought. And she still asked herself why.

Fonnie shook away the memories, turned back to Mr. Jowoski. "I've been wondering about something. Why do the nurses call you by your last name while everyone else goes by their first name?"

"Because I insist on it. I'm not going to have these young squirts call me by my first name. It leads to disrespect."

He grinned. "But you can use my first name if you wish."

"And what name would that be?"

"My friends call me Jock."

"Oh, you have friends?"

Jock cackled. "Yes. I have a few friends, and you can be one of them if you don't get too smart-assed."

"I'm thrilled with the honor. And you may call me Mrs. Beachum. Unless of course, you want to be among the young squirts who call me Fonnie."

"I detect a touch of sarcasm, Mrs. Beachum. Don't you like me?"

"I like you fine. But I don't like the way you talk to and about the nursing staff. I almost consider them family, since I'm a retired RN."

"I suppose you figure being a nurse is a holy calling."

"Not any holier than many other vocations. What about you? Did you have a holy calling?"

"Never thought of it that way. I was an attorney. And ever since Shakespeare suggested killing all the lawyers the profession has had a rough time with its public image."

"I don't know about that. I still watch an occasional rerun of Matlock and I've always admired him."

"Yes, but he's a defense attorney, freeing the wrongly accused. I, on the other hand, was a prosecuting attorney. Some folks thought I was just out to *get* people."

"Did it bother you?"

"I didn't lose any sleep over it. I did my damnedest to convict the guilty, and when I succeeded, I went for the longest sentence allowed. I usually got it. To hell with attorneys who want to mollycoddle criminals." Jock stopped for several short quick breaths. "If a man knows right from wrong and opts to do wrong, then he deserves the consequences."

Fonnie thought that over. "I guess we're not really so different. You were passionate about your work, and I was passionate about mine."

"And we both ended up here with only our memories to show for it."

"Yes," Fonnie whispered.

Jock stared at her for several seconds. Fonnie stirred uncomfortably in her wheelchair as he seemed to scrutinize her. Finally he said, "So you had a stroke?"

She nodded.

"Left side gone?"

Again she started to nod, then shook her head in the opposite direction. "Not completely. I can wiggle my fingers a bit, can even lift my left foot a fraction of an inch."

"Gonna get any better?"

"The answer to that depends on where I am on my positive-thinking thermometer. Some days I'm sure I'll walk again, and other days I wonder. Lately my thermometer readings have been abysmally low."

Jock leaned back in his chair, hooked both thumbs under his suspenders, gave them a soft snap. "At least you have a glimmer of hope." Jock licked his lips, dropped his eyes. "So are you going to ask what's wrong with me? Why I'm here? After all, I can walk and talk, and still have most of my marbles."

"No, I'm not going to ask. I think I can figure it out. It has something to do with your liver."

"Damn, you're good. How did you figure that?"

"Observation. I noticed the faint yellow hue to your nails and in the whites of your eyes." Jock nodded. "And

then you may also have a heart problem," Fonnie continued, "as evidenced by your swollen ankles. You really
should keep them elevated awhile each day."

"So now you're going to start giving me orders?"

"No. Right now I'm going to my room to check on my
roommate, Hannah. She was upset earlier about someone
she thought she'd seen. I'm sure it was just her imagination. She's probably forgotten all about it by now."

DEACON STARED INTO SPACE. He had to collect his
thoughts. All of a sudden that damned Hannah had recognized him. They'd seen each other every day since he
was admitted. He hadn't recognized her and she hadn't
seemed to know him. So what happened today to trigger
her memory? It really didn't matter. His problem now
was to do something about it. He'd waited too long,
planned too carefully to let some simpleton spoil things.
He couldn't recall who she was, but she'd shown fear
of him. She must be someone who knew him during his
troubled time. The only people he really remembered
from that time were the people responsible for his hu-
miliation. Through the years, he'd remembered and had
vowed vengeance. Only one of his enemies was still
living, and he'd tracked that person to Springwillow.
Soon he would have his revenge and it would be over.

But first he had to take care of this complication. He
knew which room was Hannah's. He'd handle the
problem—tonight.

TWO

THERE WERE TIMES when Fonnie wished her hearing had been the first to go rather than her walking ability. She could get along very nicely without hearing all that went on at Springwillow. And that included Hannah's snoring. Right now her roommate's snoring was rhythmic, soft, gurgling. It reminded Fonnie of her mother's oatmeal bubbling gently on the back burner. But Fonnie knew from last night's experience that before long the nighttime serenade would go into high gear, mimicking an asthmatic bulldozer. Fonnie scrambled around in the top drawer of her bedside stand for her earplugs. They were some she had used years ago to block out Harrison's snoring. She'd added the earplugs to her suitcase at the last minute and was now glad she had. Fonnie intended to get a good night's sleep. Since her bed was by the window, she had only to pull the privacy curtain between the two beds to shut out both Hannah and the hallway light from view. She limited her evening fluid intake so she wouldn't have to go to the bathroom during the night, and the ear plugs would muffle all noises. As the night floated by, Fonnie heard nothing, knew nothing.

FONNIE HAD LEFT HER window blinds tilted upwards so the first shafts of daylight filtered gently into the room and tickled her eyes open. As soon as she was fully awake, she flicked the call bell. Within moments, Carlotta, the night aide, appeared, pushed Fonnie's wheelchair in place and helped her to the bathroom. Another day began.

When Carlotta wheeled Fonnie out of the bathroom, the chair accidently scraped the door molding. In the quiet of the morning it grated Fonnie's nerves like a dentist drill. To her surprise, the noise didn't awaken Hannah.

"Need anything else now, Fonnie?" Carlotta asked.

"No. I'm fine. You run along. I know you're busy."

Carlotta darted down the hallway and Fonnie decided it was time for her roommate to wake up. "Come on, you lazy thing," Fonnie called out. "Up and at 'em. It's almost breakfast time." Hannah didn't stir. The curtain was still drawn and the outside light hadn't penetrated the room, so Fonnie wheeled over to the light switch. She flipped on the overhead light. The sudden glare made her momentarily blink, but when Fonnie opened her eyes again, she realized why Hannah hadn't moved.

Hannah's head was twisted awkwardly toward the door and one of her pillows lay on the bedside stand. Her lips were blue. Her right hand was tangled around her top sheet as if she'd been struggling to free herself from its clutches.

Fonnie automatically reached for Hannah's wrist to feel for a pulse. She knew she wouldn't find one.

THE DINING ROOM WAS normally a cheerful place buzzing with bits and pieces of conversation, episodes of laughter. It was furnished with sand-colored Formica-topped tables that were intended to seat four persons. However, in the mornings, most of the tables only held two or three residents since many of them preferred to eat breakfast in their rooms.

This morning the mood was somber as news of Hannah's death made the circuit. There was no formal announcement of the unexpected passing, but none was necessary. The scurrying of the nurses, the hushed whispers, the sad faces were all easily inter-preted. Fonnie was no stranger to death and it seldom spoiled her appetite. Today was different. Even the aroma of freshly brewed coffee failed to perk up her mood or her taste buds. Hannah Mullis had been a friend. True, she hadn't been a really close friend, but they had attended the same church. She and Hannah had known each other for what? Twenty years? At least twenty years.

Hannah's husband, Bill, transferred here to head the new savings and loan office, and Hannah worked in Belks' women's wear. At the time, they were empty nesters as were she and Harrison. The four of them belonged to the Good Fellowship Sunday School class of their church. They saw each other weekly and for special events. Hannah began having problems with her memory several years ago. She had to quit her job, but managed all right at home until Bill died. Then her children decided it wasn't safe for her to live alone.

When Fonnie was admitted to Springwillow, there had been two vacant beds in the facility. Fonnie didn't like the idea of sharing a room, but since she had to, she was glad it could be with someone she knew. It made little difference to Hannah. Much of the time she couldn't remember Fonnie's name, and it wasn't often that Hannah's mind was clear enough to talk about the times they'd shared. But still Hannah had been a friend and Fonnie would miss her.

Along with her sense of loss, though, Fonnie realized she also had a sense of guilt. Maybe Hannah called out to me during the night, Fonnie thought, and I didn't hear her. And if I had heard her, I might have been able to do something, at least I could have called for help. But I didn't hear anything and I didn't do anything.

Fonnie hadn't even wanted to go to breakfast, but the nurses insisted, and they banned her from her room until after the doctor made his examination and Hannah could be moved. Fonnie listened to the comments that swirled around the dining room. They were the same kind of remarks Fonnie had heard all her life. "At least now she's at peace." "She was ready to meet her maker." "But she seemed so well yesterday." "You know her heart was bad. It was only a matter of time." "Do you think she had a premonition? She seemed agitated yesterday." It was the last remark that caught Fonnie's attention. Hannah *had* been agitated and Fonnie had dismissed it as inconsequential. When she'd checked on her room-mate later in the afternoon, Hannah was calm, and had apparently forgotten about the evil man. So Fonnie forgot about him also. Now Fonnie wondered if she should have pursued the reason for Hannah's agitation.

What was it Hannah had said? Something about a man called Deacon who did bad things, and that she'd seen him. Had it been Hannah's imagination or was there really a man like that here? A dangerous man? Nonsense, Fonnie told herself as she appraised those in the dining room. Everyone here is too old, too feeble, or too addlebrained to be dangerous.

There were no assigned places in the dining room. Residents were encouraged to move around to different seats, to eat with different people. It seemed like a good idea to Fonnie, although there were some residents who claimed a particular seat as their own and dared anyone else to sit there.

Her tablemate this morning was Oliver Jefferson. He was scraggly thin and his plaid shirt hung as loose as a scarecrow's. Worry lines cascaded from the outer aspects of his eyes across sunken cheeks then joined with frown lines extending from thin, hard lips. Fonnie thought it looked as if his whole visage would crack if he attempted a smile. He introduced himself, then added, "You've probably heard of me. I seem to have acquired the nickname of Odd Oliver."

As a matter of fact, Fonnie *had* heard about him and his mania for making sure the magazines were arranged in the rack according to size with the smallest one always in front. And the day before she'd noticed him adjusting the sofa pillows so the fabric flowers were all right side up. She wasn't sure this was enough to label him as being odd, though. She extended her right hand. "I'm glad to meet you. Fonnie Beachum here."

"Too bad about Hannah. I understand you were her roommate. It must have been quite a shock to you."

"Yes, it was. So unexpected."

"Not around here. Any of us could pop off any time, you know."

Fonnie couldn't think of a comeback to that statement so she just gave her tablemate a slight nod and smile. He may be odd, but he was realistic.

While they were waiting for their trays to be served, Oliver busied himself arranging the napkin holder and the vase of plastic flowers in the exact center of the table. "I just like things to be neat and in order," he explained. "Nothing wrong with that, is there?"

"Of course not."

"Ida Mae, one of the aides, thinks I'm crazy just because I insist that my bed be made properly with the spread exactly even on both sides. She gets all jumpy when I'm in the room with her."

"I see," Fonnie said, not knowing any other comment she could make.

"Even the good book says that things should be done decently and in order."

"That's right," Fonnie said. "However, at that particular time I think the Apostle Paul was discussing how to conduct church services."

"Same difference." Oliver turned his head away and concentrated on refolding his napkin.

Fonnie realized she'd offended him, and attempted to redeem herself. "Well, as my first-grade teacher used to say, 'Neatness counts.'"

Oliver swung his head back in her direction and the corners of his lips turned up ever so slightly. "Funny you should say that. I'm a teacher myself. High-school math. You know, the thing I really like about math is that there's only one correct answer to any problem. Not like literature where the student can come up with his or her own interpretation of the author's intent. And you're right. I always insisted on neatness from my students. Sometimes I made them copy their papers over if they weren't neat—even if they had all the right answers."

Fonnie felt an instant sympathy for all his former students. She could picture them erasing any stray marks and cussing him under their breaths. She figured the only time Oliver might be dangerous was when someone deliberately hid a small magazine like *Guideposts* behind the larger *Southern Living*.

Their scrambled eggs and grits arrived. Oliver dug in with gusto, but Fonnie only played with her food while turning her attention to the other residents in the room. She was still pondering the idea that one of them could be considered dangerous.

The twins, Big and Lit Stanton, were certainly docile creatures as long as they had enough to eat. Yesterday she'd overheard Ida Mae scolding Lit about snitching

candy from the other residents' rooms. "You know
you're not allowed candy on your diabetic diet, Lit. It'll
make you sick. You don't want to get sick, do you?" Lit
shook his head and allowed the aide to open his
clenched fist. She removed the mushed nougat and
wiped his hand with a damp napkin. He seemed terribly
disappointed, but not dangerous.

She studied Lucas who was sitting at the next table
with Tillie. His face was in full view. It was a nice
looking face, rather bland but amiable. His thinning
straw-colored hair was combed neatly over a balding
spot on top. Deep grooves etched across his forehead
and on either side of his mustache.

Tillie glanced at him with adoring eyes as he
reminded her every so often to continue eating. Her
mind apparently drifted away faster than falling leaves
on a breezy day. But Lucas was so patient with her,
bringing her back to the task at hand with a gentle touch
or a soft whisper. Fonnie was surprised. Lucas had
appeared rather remote to her, but he seemed to have
taken a special liking to Tillie. Fonnie thought the situation was rather sweet.

Then there was Jock: blustery, mouthy, breathing out
empty threats, but dangerous? No, certainly not. And
cultured, traveled, handsome Calvin. Fonnie hadn't had
a chance to get acquainted with him yet, but she was
anxious to do so. The only danger he posed, Fonnie
thought, was the danger of becoming too good a friend.
The thought surprised and pleased her. Although the

stroke had been devastating, it hadn't destroyed any really vital instincts.

After breakfast, Keisha pushed Fonnie into the day room. Keisha had quickly become Fonnie's favorite aide. Her wiry black hair topped a bronze, lanky body with strong arms and gentle hands. But most importantly she had an incurable smile that seldom failed to lift Fonnie's spirits.

Fonnie could propel herself for short distances by lifting up the right footrest and using her foot like an oar while her right hand worked the wheel. But it was a laborious process and usually the aides found it much easier to get her out of their way by doing it themselves.

Keisha deposited Fonnie in front of the TV where Diane Sawyer was interviewing a sobbing victim of some crime or disaster. Fonnie was in no mood for victims this morning.

"How about shoving me over to the window? I'd love to see some sign of spring, if such a thing exists."

"Oh, there is. The daffodils are about gone but there's some red trillium blooming, and some phlox." Keisha pulled back heavy drapes that blanketed the window, and shook her head. "But I'm afraid you can't see the flower bed from here. If I have time later, I'll take you outside for a bit. Sorry I can't do it now."

Fonnie was sorry also. She longed for her flower bed at home, to feel the damp earth between her fingers, to smell the promise of spring blossoms. Last year at this time she was planting anemones and pink dahlias. Her dogwood trees were covered with tiny pearls and the other trees were wearing gowns of fuzzy green. She took a deep breath imagining fresh spring air. She immediately started choking. The housekeeper was spraying air-freshener around the room with the zest of a crop duster spraying for weevils. The can was labeled "Country Garden." The closest that vile spray ever came to a country garden, Fonnie thought, was when the farmer spread out fresh manure.

Fonnie wheeled herself along the wall and backed into a space beside a rubber tree plant.

The new greenery had been distributed throughout the various rooms used by the residents: the day room, of course, but also the dining room, computer room and chapel. Fonnie liked the effect. It not only brought some nature in, but the plants divided the large rooms into smaller, more intimate areas.

As Fonnie was maneuvering her chair out of the way of traffic, she brushed against the bulletin board. This was the official administration board posting the residents rights and obligations. A smiling face, identified as the area ombudsman, beamed benignly from the board, along with a telephone number where residents could report grievances. Another notice listed the state hotline number. Fonnie had paid scant attention to the board in the past, but as she tried to move her wheelchair, she noticed a new attachment. The fact that it was hand printed instead of the usual typed memorandums caught her interest. The notice was just slightly above her eye level. She tilted her head, adjusted her bifocals, and read the message. The bold block letters proclaimed, I AM ALPHA AND OMEGA, THE BEGINNING AND THE END.

Fonnie briefly wondered why someone felt compelled to post such a note. Maybe it was the emphasis being given to making the nursing home a replica of Eden, the supposed place of man's beginnings. Although some would disagree, Fonnie figured the first Eden was as good a beginning for us earthlings as any other place. And, her brain conceded, this Eden was probably as good a place as any to meet our end. This sobering thought brought her mind back to Hannah.

At the same time Fonnie saw Jean and Dr. Whitcomb come down the hallway to the nurses' station. Jean handed him a chart. He flopped into a chair, turned some pages in the chart and started scribbling.

Fonnie studied the doctor she'd known and worked with at the hospital. She was surprised he was still in active practice. He must be nearly as old as I am, she thought. He looked tired: tired from years of work, tired from years of caring, tired from years of pronouncing people dead.

She wondered if he would remember her. She scooted her chair closer to the door so she could catch his attention on his way out. Fonnie wanted to find out what he had written as the cause of Hannah's death.

"Dr. Whitcomb." The doctor strode on by, placed his hand on the doorknob. Fonnie tried again, this time a little louder. "Dr. Whitcomb, may I talk to you a minute?"

The doctor swung his stooped shoulders around, squinted at the old woman in the wheelchair. "Yes? What can I do for you?"

"Remember me? I'm Fonnie Beachum. From the hospital."

Dr. Whitcomb shook his head. "Um-mm. I'm sorry. I can't place you right now. Were you one of my patients?"

Fonnie grinned. "Not exactly. Maybe you'd remember if I was wearing a white uniform, and had a stethoscope around my neck."

The doctor's lips slid in a professional smile. "Of course. Fonnie. My favorite nurse. You retired much too soon. The hospital needs nurses like you."

"I'm afraid nobody needs me anymore. Not in my condition."

Dr. Whitcomb perked up his smile and patted her arm. "Just keep your chin up. I'm sure you'll make a good recovery."

"Thanks for the pep talk, but that's not why I stopped you. Hannah was my roommate and I want to know what happened to her."

Dr. Whitcomb spread out his hands as if that explained everything, and then said, "Her heart, of course. It just gave out."

"Are you sure? I mean, she didn't even ring her call bell for help. She would have had some warning, some pain before the end."

"She probably did, but her mind wasn't able to respond to the warning." The doctor patted Fonnie's arm again.

"Don't worry. She didn't suffer. The end was quick." He took a deep breath. "Something we all could wish for."

"You're not going to get an autopsy?"

"Whatever for? She's at peace now, Fonnie. Let her rest."

After the doctor left, Fonnie tried to do just that, but she couldn't let her thoughts of Hannah rest. It was sad that poor Hannah, who seldom remembered anything, had her last day on earth marred by a bad memory from the past. And why, Fonnie wondered again, did her friend suddenly remember a man called Deacon and his actions? Fonnie pondered on this while Hannah's body was being removed.

Fonnie knew that traumatic events could etch themselves on a person's brain deeper than ordinary happenings. And that we're more apt to recall incidents from our youth than from later life. It made sense then, if Deacon really existed, that he was from Hannah's younger years.

Fonnie remembered now that Hannah had called him a boy, and said it was a long time ago. Was he responsible for some traumatic event in her early life? Did her fear of him induce a fatal heart attack? Or had something more sinister happened? And who was Deacon?

DEACON WATCHED from a secluded corner as Hannah's body, covered by a white sheet, was quietly wheeled down the hall and out the back door. It had been so simple—a pillow over her face for a few minutes. Of course, he'd been cautious. He'd waited until the middle of the night and made sure the RN on duty and one aide were on the skilled nursing end of the hall. He knew they would be busy there for some time. The other aide, left at the desk to answer call lights, was busy copying something into a notebook. She wouldn't notice anything. Earlier in the day, he had scouted out the room, was pleased to see her name on the bed nearest the door. Perfect.

He'd kept thinking about this Hannah throughout the afternoon and then it dawned on him who she was. She'd been in that group from the junior college. The group that had turned against him. Well, she's paid for it now. There was only one more left who had tormented him back then. And that one would soon pay also.

THREE

THE ARRIVAL OF the cats and Fonnie's haircut were scheduled for the same morning as Hannah's death. But life had to go on. Fonnie tried to put Hannah and Deacon, if there really was such a person, out of her mind to concentrate on the two forthcoming events. She looked forward to the first event with happy anticipation and with dread to the other.

Ginger, the activities director, whose personality was as spicy as her name, was busy coaxing and wheeling residents into the day room. The area was nearly full, not only with most of the regulars, but with several residents who seldom left their rooms. Fonnie stayed in the background and studied the residents she hadn't seen before. There was a handsome black man whose right pant leg was folded under and pinned just below his knee, and a hefty Hispanic woman who kept muttering something to the aides that either they ignored or couldn't understand. Some of the women had brought their knitting or cross stitching. Some faces were eager, others confused, and others blank.

Fonnie noted that Jock was nowhere to be seen. His favorite chair was conspicuously empty. She wasn't surprised that he was absent. But she was surprised that no one had claimed his chair.

Everyone in the day room waited eagerly for the new arrivals. Ginger went out to her van parked in front of the home and brought in two cat carriers. Fonnie craned her neck to get a glimpse of the felines.

Ginger did the introductions. "This one is Sheba," she said as she reached for a striped tabby in shades of butter yellow and biscuit brown with a white bib under its chin. Sheba, however, was in no hurry to meet her many admirers. She tried to latch one paw onto the swinging door and another one onto the sleeve of Ginger's sweat suit. But since the cat had been declawed, she didn't have much staying power. Ginger unwrapped both paws, and stroked the cat's back, that was beginning to arch. "Now Sheba, this is your new home and these are your new friends. So you behave yourself. Understand?" Ginger went part way around the room, showing Sheba off and allowing the residents to rub the soft fur and greet her in kitty talk.

Fonnie could tell that Sheba was beginning to relax and enjoy the attention. That is until they reached the chair where Tillie sat. Maybe Tillie stretched out her hand a little too quickly or jerkily to suit Sheba. Whatever the reason, Sheba arched up, hissed a bad word, and snapped sharp teeth at Tillie's middle finger. Tillie jerked her hand away before Sheba could do any damage, but tears sprang to the woman's eyes and her hands shook. Fonnie wheeled over closer. "It's all right," she assured Tillie. "We'll pet the cat later." Tillie nodded, but kept wary eyes on Sheba as Ginger continued parading her around the room.

When they reached the Stanton twins, Lit reached out to take Sheba in his arms. Ginger carefully deposited Sheba in Lit's lap and stood back. Lit reached up to his shirt pocket and pulled out a crumpled napkin. He quickly opened the napkin, pored out some bits of bacon into his hand and offered Sheba the tasty treat. Sheba succumbed to the bribery, and Lit made a friend.

With Sheba in good hands, Ginger opened the other carrier. "And this stately gentleman is King Tut." Fonnie smiled as King Tut strutted out of the cage, head held high, every glossy Persian gray hair in place. The cat surveyed his subjects, gave a low purr and flounced over to the empty green chair. Daring anyone to stop him, Tut vaulted into the soft cushion and staked his claim. Oh, oh, Fonnie thought. She knew a battle could be in the offing when Jock came in. But she was inclined to put her money on the king.

Several minutes later, Keisha interrupted Fonnie's enjoyment of the cat show. "The beautician's ready for you. I'll push you down."

"Thanks. Might as well get it over with." Fonnie tried her best to resuscitate her sense of humor that seemed to have been mortally wounded in the aftermath of her stroke. "I know exactly how I want my hair," she said to the aide.

"And how is that?"

"Just like yours. Short and kinky. Then I'll never have another bad hair day."

Keisha giggled. "Fonnie, you can get it cut as short as you like, but you don't have the genes for kinky. My ancestors worked hard for this hair and we don't give it away to white folks."

"Then I'll settle for second best—a tight perm. Maybe even some color. What do you think about a reddish tint? You know, my hair used to be the color of a copper kettle."

"I'll go for that. No use you going around looking like a snowball."

THE BEAUTICIAN'S NAME was Glenda. She had a big mouth, a bigger laugh, warm eyes, and long, slender fingers. She was twirling a curling iron and telling a joke as Keisha wheeled Fonnie through the door. "So the doctor tells the patient that she needs an oophorectomy. 'You must be wrong, Doc,' the woman says, 'it's been years since I've had any oomph.'"

Glenda hew hawed at her own cleverness, Fonnie and Keisha laughed heartily and the other two ladies in the room looked puzzled. Finally the one whose hair was being fried said, "I don't get it."

Keisha stopped laughing and tried to explain. "Well, you see, an oophorectomy is when an ovary is removed, but the patient thought the doctor was going to remove her oomph." Keisha's explanation was met by two blank stares.

"Never mind," Glenda said. "It really wasn't all that funny." The beautician turned to greet the newcomer. "You must be Fonnie. Welcome to Fantasy Land where all the women are beautiful and wishes come true every day."

Keisha parked Fonnie in the corner. "Fonnie, this lovely creature is Glenda the Great. She's right up there next to the Fairy Godmother when it comes to performing miracles."

Fonnie pushed her glasses up, grinned at the aide. "Are you implying that I need a miracle?"

Keisha smiled. "Just a wee one."

"Get gone, Keisha," Glenda said. "The next time you see Fonnie, she'll be a new woman." Keisha scooted out the door. Glenda asked, "Fonnie have you met these other lovely ladies?"

Fonnie shook her head, and wondered which one of the women had splashed herself with Lilly of the Valley cologne. Fonnie pulled a tissue from her pocket and blew her nose. The action did little to block out the cloying scent.

Glenda spun one last curl on the woman in her chair. "This is Maude. She's a champion with crochet needles. She makes doll clothes and afghans."

Maude acknowledged the introduction with a nod of her head and a satisfied smile. "I also make bead necklaces." She fingered the multicolored beads encircling her wizened neck. "Like them?"

"Yes. They're lovely," Fonnie said, and hoped Maude wouldn't take the forced compliment too seriously.

Glenda waved her comb to the other corner. "And over there, waiting for a comb-out, is Alfreda. She paints fantastic birdhouses." Alfreda grinned at the acclamation.

"I'm so pleased to meet both of you," Fonnie said. "I've seen you in the dining room, in the far corner with two other ladies."

Alfreda nodded. "Dora and Rachel. We four always eat together. Jean calls us the Four Musketeers. I know we're supposed to circulate, but we enjoy each other. Why mess up a good thing?"

"Makes sense to me. But where do you spend the rest of your time? I haven't seen you in the day room."

"Ginger keeps us busy in the craft room," Maude answered. "Several of us are working on a quilt right now. We plan to raffle it off later. We need money to buy more supplies."

"And I'm going to sell my birdhouses," Alfreda added. "You ought to come join us. You'll enjoy it."

Fonnie shook her head. "I never was one to do crafts and I guess now it's too late. Can't do much with only one hand."

Glenda laughed. "You'd be surprised. Ginger has quite a bag of tricks. She'd find something for you to do."

"Maybe later. Right now I'll just enjoy Ginger's cats. I think Sheba and I will become good friends."

Glenda's nimble fingers kept working during all the chatter. She finished Maude with a quick puff of hair spray and started on Alfreda. Glenda's smile faded. "You know, Hannah would have enjoyed the cats. She was always so chipper. She may not have known what day it was, but she delighted in whatever was going on."

Maude agreed. "She'd come down to the craft room most afternoons and just stand around and smile." Then Maude frowned. "Come to think of it, she didn't come down yesterday at all. I wonder why."

Fonnie made no comment. She knew why Hannah hadn't made her visit to the craft room, but she didn't want to discuss it.

Glenda put the finishing touches on Alfreda's hair, and the two women turned to go. "Now do come down to the craft room, Fonnie," Alfreda said. "We'll find something for you to do."

"And try to get Calvin or Oliver to come down with you," Maude said. "I've invited them several times, but they won't come. Maybe you could get them to change their minds. We certainly could use some male company. Especially Calvin. He's so handsome."

Alfreda shook her head. "'Handsome is as handsome does,' my mother used to say, and I'm not so sure we want handsome Calvin in the craft room."

Glenda's penciled eyebrows shut up. "Why ever not? You know something the rest of us don't know?"

"All I know is that he spends an awful lot of time in the computer room and I just bet he's in there looking at dirty pictures. What else would he be doing?"

"You mean Internet porn?" Glenda scratched the back of her neck. "Well, that's one way to keep up to date with what's going on in the world. What's the harm?"

"You might think there's no harm in it, but I, for one, will not associate with fornicators." Alfreda gave a righteous sniff as she headed out the door. "And believe me, I've seen the way he leers at the young nurses. I don't want to have anything to do with him."

Maude winked at Glenda and Fonnie as she followed her friend out. "I don't think you need to worry, dear. If I can get him to the craft room, he'll be too busy helping me with the quilt to be leering at you."

Maude and Alfreda shuffled down the hall and Glenda helped Fonnie switch chairs. "Now tell me what you want."

Fonnie explained just how she wanted her hair done. Glenda demurred when Fonnie mentioned coloring. "It's better to wait a week after a perm before putting color on," she explained to Fonnie.

"I know, but I want it all done today. If I wait, I may change my mind."

ABOUT TWO HOURS LATER Fonnie left the beauty shop— cut, curled and colored. It was lunchtime so Keisha pushed her into the dining room. She saw Maude and Alfreda and their table mates across the room. They all smiled at her and nodded their heads in approval.

The only place left open was across the table from Jock Jowoski. Jock took one look at her and broke into a grin that displayed every tooth in his head. "Hoot, gal. You've done it now. No one will ever mistake you for a sweet old lady again. Of course, folks are apt to wonder how you ended up with cotton candy on your head, but that's all right. I like it." He reached over to her wheelchair, patted her arm. "Don't you fret none. I'll keep Lit away from you if he gets to thinking your head is something good to eat."

Fonnie tried to keep a straight face. "You know, when I heard a strange noise I thought it was Harrison rolling over in his grave. But now I see it was just you drooling over my beauty."

"That's right. I may even nominate you for Queen of the Jungle. How are you with swinging on vines?"

"A little out of practice, I'm afraid." Fonnie patted the fuzz over her right ear. "I just hope Amy likes it as much as you do. Maybe I'd better e-mail her this afternoon so when she comes it won't be a complete surprise."

After lunch Jock pushed Fonnie out to the day room, and then headed for his favorite chair. Fortunately, King Tut had abandoned his throne to play tag with Sheba among the potted plants. Fonnie noticed that Tut had left a batch of gray hair to mark his province, but Jock either didn't notice or didn't care. He dropped down and picked up the latest issue of *Newsweek*.

Fonnie picked up the nearest magazine and flipped the pages with her right hand. She used to love reading *Better Homes and Gardens* with its pictures and how-to sections, but now it was irrelevant. This was her home and she had no say in how it was decorated. The only say-so she had left in life was over half a room and part of her body. She patted her hair again and was pleased with the soft texture, the tight curls, and remembered with delight how the Flaming Sunset rinse shone in the mirror. She glanced around the room, hoped someone would come up and comment on her new do. No one did. Everyone was busy in his or her own little world.

Gwendolyn, in her plaid pant suit and sensible black loafers, was engrossed in *All My Children*. Lucas was scrunched down in the corner of the brown sofa, his feet pushed as far back as they would go, and his face hidden in a large-print issue of *Guideposts*. Tillie was busy tying and untying the hair bow on her baby doll. Calvin was nowhere in sight.

The twins, Big and Lit, sat in front of a jigsaw puzzle of Pinocchio. Big grinned as he showed Lit a piece of Pinocchio's nose. Ginger always kept two puzzles going: a thousand-piece one for avid puzzlers and a hundred-piece one for dabblers and those with short attention spans. The twins were definitely dabblers.

Fonnie had known the Stanton twins all their lives. They were born in the hospital where she worked fifty years ago. They were premature, but mature enough to survive. The birth was difficult though, and apparently the babies had suffered some anoxia in the process. The lack of oxygen may have been the cause of their limited mental capacity. In spite of, or maybe because of, their handicaps, the twins were loved, coddled, spoiled. They were given the proper names of Harold and Howard, but people seldom used them. The bigger one was called Big and the littler one was Lit. They both, though, had

large frames and corpulent bodies. Big was the brighter
of the two, and therefore he was very protective of his
brother. They were placed in the nursing home after
their parents died, and the staff at Springwillow became
their guardians. Everyone loved them, and Fonnie had
been told that until recently they'd been allowed to roam
freely. Then Lit was diagnosed with diabetes and the
staff had to curb his appetite and his roaming. But he
soon became an expert at finding contraband sweets in
both the kitchen and other residents' rooms.

Fonnie decided she needed to check her e-mail for
messages, and to send one to Amy. There was no aide in
sight, so she did what she termed her "wheelie shuffle"
and headed for the computer room. As she passed the
bulletin board, she noticed another unauthorized memo.
The previous one about Alpha and Omega had been torn
down, and Fonnie hoped this one would soon follow. It
was written in the same black block letters. VEN-
GEANCE IS MINE. I WILL REPAY. Fonnie winced as
she scooted past. She couldn't imagine who would write
and post such a message or why. Was it meant as a
warning? Or was it some kind of sick joke? She tried to
put it out of her mind as she made her way down the hall.

Fonnie was pleased to find she had an e-mail from
Amy. *Good news. Brian is giving up his Myrtle Beach
spring break to spend time with us. Will wonders never
cease? He'll come home and then we'll both drive down
to see you. I'll let you know dates, times later. And Mom,
we have to talk about the house.*

Of course they had to talk about the house. The house where Amy grew up, the house where Brian learned to walk during the time he and Amy lived there following her divorce, the house that echoed with loneliness after Harrison's death. On the whole it had been a happy house, good memories crammed into every corner. Amy probably thought her mother was going to protest selling the house and had convinced Brian to come along for reinforcement. Well, I'm not going to put up an argument, Fonnie thought. No one has to tell me now that it's time to let go.

Fonnie fired off her own e-mail. She didn't mention the house. Let Amy stew a little. It'd do her good. *Dear Amy, Will be so glad to see Brian. Is he bringing a girl? Got my hair cut this morning. Now I can brush it myself. I'm going for PT evaluation this afternoon. I hear they've hired a new therapist—described as a "hunk"—can't wait to try walking again. Love, Mom.*

"THIS IS GOING TO BE harder than I thought," Deacon muttered to himself. "I have the stuff, but how to do it?" Deacon rubbed his jaw. Making sure the hallway was clear and that no one was apt to enter his room, Deacon went to the closet and hauled out one brown dress shoe. He loosened the laces, reached his hand into the toe section, and brought out a plastic sandwich bag. He smiled. The white powder in the bag looked harmless enough. Anyone seeing it might think he kept a stash of baking soda on hand to take for indigestion. But the

powder was far from harmless. A few teaspoonsful
mixed with orange juice or iced tea would be a deadly
cocktail. His intended victim, however, wasn't likely to
accept a drink from him, or even a tainted cookie. But
he had to find a way. It had taken him weeks to accu-
mulate enough pentobarbital to be a fatal dose. Every
night at bedtime, the nurse came in with the sleeping pill
and a smile. He'd smile back, place the capsule in his
mouth—in his cheek to be more exact—take a swallow
of water, thank the nurse. She'd leave and he'd retrieve
the capsule from his mouth, open it up and pour the
white powder into the sandwich bag.

He sighed and carefully replaced the bag in the toe
of the shoe. As he shoved the shoe back in the closet, a
new thought crept into his mind. Maybe I'm thinking
too small. Maybe one more victim isn't enough. After
all, in a way, they're all responsible. No one ever understood me. And they still don't. In their eyes, I'm nothing.
They all should be damned to hellfire. Especially that
hussy that cut her hair. She looked decent before that.
Now she's just another whore—just like Mama.

He remembered how his mama curled up her hair
before going out, telling him to get to bed, and not to
dare breathe a word to his daddy when he came home—
if his daddy took a notion to come home at all. Of course,
one night he did come home, and caught her coming in,
dress all torn, hair all mussed. Daddy was right. Just a
beating was too good for her. She deserved nothing less
than hellfire. And that's what she got. Daddy sent him

off to live with Maw Maw before the fire. They called it an accident, but he knew. It was vengeance, justice. And both he and Daddy slept better after that. Nothing like vengeance to make for sound sleeping.

Maybe that was why he hadn't been sleeping well lately. These hands were God's hands and he'd been slack in performing His duties. Well, he'd correct that. And perhaps the pentobarbital wasn't such a good idea, after all. A fire would be simpler—and would take care of all of them at once.

FOUR

FONNIE GLANCED AT the wall clock. It was getting close to her PT appointment, and she had neither the time nor the strength to wheel herself all the way from the computer room to the physical therapy room. She looked around for a call bell to summon someone to push her down the halls. She couldn't find one. This annoyed her. Every room was supposed to have at least one call bell. There had to be one here someplace. She shuffled back and forth along the row of computers, checked near the light switch, finally spotted the bell hidden behind the leaves of a newly placed Ficus plant. The plant was lovely, but, she thought, it would have to be moved. She made a mental note to mention it to Ginger or Jean.

Fonnie shoved aside some leaves and gave the black button a hearty push. She was rewarded with a gentle, "ping, ping, ping," and a flashing light above the outside of the door. She knew a corresponding light would be flashing at the control board at the nurses' station. Her transportation should be arriving soon.

It was Ida Mae who stepped through the door, turned the call bell off, smiled when she saw Fonnie. "I'm so glad it's you," she said. "I was afraid it was going to be that creepy Calvin. He spends so much time down here."

"Why do you think he's creepy? Calvin strikes me as a very nice gentleman."

"I just don't like the way he looks at me—kind of spooky."

"Nonsense. You're young and pretty. Men like that—nothing spooky about it."

"Well, anyway, I'm here to do your bidding. Where to, Madam?"

As Fonnie and Ida Mae passed the craft room, they heard a babble of voices, giggles, and squeals. "Sounds like the ladies are enjoying themselves," Fonnie said.

"They usually do. Sometimes they act like a bunch of schoolkids." Fonnie squirmed in her wheelchair. She didn't want to act like a schoolkid. She just wanted to get back to being a fully functioning adult.

The physical therapy room was dark. Ida Mae switched on a light by the door. It's thin rays only slightly illuminated the cavernous room, creating ominous shadows in the background. "I'm sure the therapist will be here shortly," Ida Mae said. "You don't mind if I leave, do you? I have scads of work to do."

Fonnie put on a brave face. "I don't mind. You run along. I'll be fine."

Ida Mae skipped out of the room. Fonnie stared at the army of exercise equipment looming like monsters before her. She knew their thoughts. They were scoffing at her audacity to think she might conquer any one of them. Their siblings had defeated her before and now they were ready to take up the battle.

Fonnie's right hand reached down to turn the wheel-chair around and flee her enemies. A soft voice stopped her. "Sorry I'm late."

Fonnie gazed at the man who blocked her path of escape. The physical therapist was indeed a hunk. He was basketball-player tall with weight-lifter muscles and raven-black hair slicked back like Wayne Newton in Las Vegas. He wore a tight scrub suit of cerulean blue, the same color as his eyes, and his smile looked as if he was hiding a delicious secret. The fact that he was forty years younger than she, did nothing to deter Fonnie from finding him enchanting. *Maybe I was a little hasty,* she thought, *in thinking my paralyzed limbs are hope-less. This fellow might be just the person to bring them back to life.*

Fonnie looked around defiantly at the equipment: the stationary bikes, the parallel walking bars, the varying sets of weights, the treadmill, the whirlpool. "All this for me?" she asked the therapist.

"Perhaps. I'll do an evaluation and figure out just what you need, Mrs. Beachum." His voice was low and husky with a Southern drawl which extended her name to, "Bea-a-chum," making it sound like something good to eat.

"Everyone here calls me 'Fonnie.'"

"Fo-on-nie," he said, drawing the name out to three syllables. "Lovely name. Is it short for something?"

"No. It's my real name, an old-fashioned Southern

name. It's been handed down in my mother's family for generations."

"So glad to meet you, Fo-on-nie. I'm Andy." He bent toward her, took both her hands, and turned them palms up. For a wild second Fonnie thought he might be going to actually kiss them, but she soon realized he was just starting his evaluation of her physical status. The fingers of her right hand bent slightly upward, tense, ready for whatever command her mind would give it. Her left hand lay limp, flaccid, useless. He flexed her weakened fingers, squeezed them, and gave her a smile of encouragement.

Andy was meticulous in his examination and in documenting the findings. Fonnie was glad. She knew Medicare regulations were strict and that they would approve payment for physical therapy only if there was documented hope for improvement. When Andy finished, she waited quietly for his decision. Would he try to help her? Or would he say there was no use?

Andy frowned, pulled on his right ear, nodded his head slightly. "We'll try it for six weeks. Three times a week. Hopefully there'll be enough improvement to justify continuing."

"And if there's not?"

"Then I'll prescribe maintenance exercises that the aides can do. But Fo-on-nie, we're not going there yet. You and I have a lot of work to do."

It's a good thing I'm a fighter, Fonnie thought. *And there's nothing like a handsome man to make the fight worthwhile.*

FONNIE WAS TIRED after leaving the exercise room and decided to take a nap. She hailed Ida Mae for a ride back to her room. Ida Mae was a little chubby and a lot bouncy, especially her hair and her boobs. With every step the front of her uniform rose and fell like incoming ocean waves, and her blond curls romped around the rims of her gold-framed glasses. Fonnie liked Ida Mae, but had to restrain herself from suggesting that the aide invest in a firm sports bra and some hair spray.

When they reached her room, Fonnie stretched out on top of the spread, pulled the afghan over her legs, and closed her eyes. She was just dozing off when she heard footsteps. Fonnie squinted toward the door. If it was somebody she didn't want to see, she'd pretend to be asleep. But she recognized Hannah's son and slid up to a sitting position.

"I'm sorry. I didn't mean to disturb you, Mrs. Beachum. I just came by to pick up Mother's things. The nurses had packed up everything, but I thought I'd drop in and say hello."

"I'm glad you did, Harry. I was hoping to see some of the family. I'm so sorry about your mother. I know it was a shock."

"Well, not really. We knew she had a bad heart. The doctor said she didn't suffer. I guess that's the best way to go. And of course, it's not like she's been herself for quite a few years now."

"Yes. She had her good days and bad days. But most

of the time she seemed pretty content." Fonnie wondered if she should mention Hannah's agitation the evening before her death. Would her son know anything about Deacon? She decided to give it a try. "You know, your mother sometimes talked about her younger days, but I could only get bits and pieces of it. Where did she live as a child? Was it in the mountains?"

"The foothills, actually. Several miles south of Boone. She met Dad in Charlotte and they lived there several years."

"Did she keep in touch with her old friends?" Fonnie noticed the odd look Harry gave her as he shook his head, but she kept going. "It's just that she mentioned a friend to me the other day. I assumed he was from her high school or college days. I think she said his name was Deacon. It stuck in my mind because it was an unusual name. Do you know anything about him?"

Harry shook his head again. "No. No, I never heard that name before. But it's strange, she seldom spoke of her past or when she was young, and she never seemed to want to go back home to visit. I remember one summer, our whole family took a trip to Asheville and the surrounding area. When we came back, we drove up the Blue Ridge Parkway and then down 321. We asked Mom if she wanted to stop by her old home place, but she didn't want to. She said that when she was growing up, there was nothing there except moonshine and cock fights, and that she doubted it had improved any.

As far as I know she never did go back." Harry paused. "I wonder if there was something she didn't want to remember."

"Perhaps. But I guess it doesn't matter now." Fonnie extended her hand. "It was good to see you. Say hello to your sisters for me. I'm sorry I won't be able to attend the funeral."

AFTER SUPPER Fonnie entered the day room just in time to witness the first skirmish between Jock and King Tut. Tut was curled up to the size of a pair of earmuffs, snoozing peacefully in the overstuffed chair. Jock glared at the intruder, rolled up the newspaper he had in his hand and sent Tut hurling into space. True to cat nature, the king landed on all fours. He shook his head and seemed to be debating a counterattack when Gwendolyn's eager hands swooped him up.

"Never mind that mean old man, Tutty. You come to me. My lap is bigger and softer than any shabby chair." With that pronouncement, Gwendolyn collapsed on the sofa and her lap cascaded around her middle like a punctured inner tube. She plopped King Tut somewhere between her knees and her navel and the cat disappeared. He managed to lift his head up enough to breathe and extended one paw in thanks. They then both turned their attention to *Wheel of Fortune*.

Fonnie scooted her wheelchair closer to Jock. "Congratulations. Round one goes to you. But I'm not counting King Tut out yet."

"Drat cat! And the nurse said they wouldn't bother me. Hmph."

"Oh, forget about the cat," Fonnie blurted out. "I need some intelligent conversation for a change. Unfortunately, there's not much of that floating around."

Jock seemed to relent, put down his newspaper, and studied her. "It's been hard on you, gal, hasn't it?" Fonnie nodded and breathed deeply to keep back tears. "I know how it is," Jock said. "After a lifetime of cerebral activity, we're suddenly dumped into a mental vacuum. Our greatest challenge now is deciding between orange juice and prunes for breakfast."

"How do you stand it?"

"By being grouchy." Jock gave her a wicked grin. "Or haven't you noticed?"

"Oh, I've noticed. You've elevated grouchy to an art form. And since I can't compete with you, I'll have to find another outlet." Fonnie patted her new curls, gazed around the room. "Some people write their memoirs when they're our age. Ever thought about it?"

"Nope. Most of my life was spent in a courtroom sending people to prison, and most of them I'd just as soon forget."

"You never married? Children?"

"Yes, I was married twice—both briefly and without offspring. So you see, I really don't have much to write. My childhood was dull and though I wouldn't call my career dull, it's nothing anyone would want to read about."

"And where did you spend this dull childhood and career?"

"Western North Carolina—from Asheville to Boone to Hickory and spots in between. Anything else you want to know, Miss Nosy?"

"No. That about covers it." Fonnie rested her chin on her right hand. "Oh, except for one more thing. Did you ever know Hannah before you and she arrived here?"

Jock frowned. "What is this? An inquisition? Or are your memoirs going to include everyone else here?"

"No. Of course not. I just happened to think of Hannah because she had mentioned seeing someone from her college days."

"Well, I went to Davidson. I have no idea where Hannah went—or even if she did go to college." Jock picked up the newspaper. "Now if you'll excuse me, I'll occupy my brain by reading all the terrible news of the world."

But Fonnie's mind had taken a sharp curve, and she didn't even notice she had been dismissed. "You know what I miss even more than cerebral challenges?" Her voice took on a distant tone and her eyes turned upward, following the flights of the wallpaper butterflies.

Jock's face softened. He dropped the paper and reached for her hand. "And what would that be?"

"Dancing. I'll never dance again." Her eyes met his. "I loved dancing."

Jock cleared his throat, patted her hand, and looked away.

LATER WHEN HE WAS in his room, Deacon sat thinking and scribbling. His plans had changed, had expanded, but he had to work out the details. It wouldn't be easy. This damn home was built to comply with all the safety codes: sprinkler systems, smoke detectors, security system. The sprinklers were a special problem. No fire he could set would last long with buckets of water falling down. But he knew how to disengage them, along with the smoke alarms. It's amazing the things one learns while traveling through life.

As he thought, he scribbled. He drew diagrams of the rooms. He drew pretty flames devouring the curtains in the day room, flames soaring up in the laundry, flames attacking the rooms of his enemies. It would be a beautiful spectacle.

His thoughts were interrupted by spicy little Ginger. "Bingo in ten minutes. Want to join us?"

Why not? Maybe getting his mind off the problem for a few minutes would clear his thoughts. Then he could come back and work on the details. "Be right out." He folded the drawings carefully and arranged them in his bedside table drawer under his electric razor. He then placed two candy bars on top of the razor. A volunteer from one of the local churches had given him the candy this morning from what she called her "goodie cart." After making sure his name wasn't on the list of residents who couldn't have candy, she thrust two Milky Ways into his hands. He saved them to enjoy later. He'd smiled when she came to Lit and he tried to grab a candy bar from her cart. The church lady knew Lit wasn't allowed candy so she handed him an apple instead. In return Lit gave her a dirty look. Deacon hurried out to join the bingo players, thinking his secret plans and his candy bars were safe.

FIVE

THE BINGO TABLE commandeered the distant side of the day room, far enough away so the game wouldn't interfere with TV viewers. Fonnie watched Ginger position the players around the table and admired the way the young girl related so well with all the residents. She encouraged the timid ones, calmed the overzealous, admired a pretty dress, commented on a pleasant aftershave lotion, smiled indiscriminately. Ginger must be on a flexible schedule, Fonnie thought, to accommodate all the activities she does.

Ginger motioned Fonnie to a vacant space between Alfreda and a black lady whose name Fonnie couldn't remember. The table was soon full with eager faces and ready hands. The many prizes were stacked on a card table nearby. Most of the prizes were inexpensive and practical: shampoos, tissues, combs and brushes, colognes, stationery. Interspersed with these were a few more highly desirable awards such as pillow dolls with pretty crocheted dresses, and paperback novels— westerns for the men and romances for the women. Fonnie remembered years ago her Sunday School class used to donate items for these bingo games. Now it was her turn to be on the receiving end. The thought nearly nauseated her. She took two deep breaths and forced a smile. This must be what Shakespeare meant, Fonnie thought, when he said something like, "life is time's fool."

Calvin sat right across from her and he must have thought the smile was for him because he beamed back. "Glad you decided to join us tonight, Fonnie. Feel lucky?"

"Not exactly."

"Well, I am. I have my eye on a Louie L'Amour book."

Jock was sitting two chairs down from Calvin between Maude and Dora. "Why, Cal," Jock said, "I had you pegged more for Danielle Steele. And I bet Lucas would love to get his hands on one of those Kewpie dolls."

Calvin winced. Lucas kept his head down, but Fonnie could tell he was clenching his teeth. Oliver looked up from aligning his cards to the edge of the table and yelled out, "Damn it, Jock. Shut that big trap of yours. Did you come here to play bingo or to insult people?"

"Well, if I had come here to insult people, I'd start with you, Miss Prissy. Who in the hell cares if your cards are in exactly the right position? You're enough to drive a person batty."

Oliver pushed his chair back from the table, his spindly frame wobbled, his hands shook. "You take that back. You—you—Neanderthal!"

Silence hovered over the table. Eyes darted between Oliver and Jock. The two men reminded Fonnie of schoolboys just itching for a fight. No one said anything, but Fonnie suspected that sides were being taken and silent bets were being placed on the combatants. Fonnie could sense disappointment scooting around the table when Jock let out a barrel laugh and then apologized. "Sorry about that, Roomie. Don't know what came over me."

Oliver grinned back. "That's okay. I knew you were just messing with me."

Fonnie gaped at the two of them. "You two are roommates? I didn't know that."

Jock nodded. "We actually get along very nicely. I just stir him up once in a while when things get boring. But we never go to bed mad. Do we, Oliver?"

"That's right. Our nights are peaceful. Of course that's because Jock takes sleeping pills, and I take out my hearing aid, so we both sleep like babies."

Ginger smiled and twirled the bingo numbers around. "Let the games begin."

Fonnie played, but her mind really wasn't in it. She spent more time in studying her fellow residents than thinking about her card. She'd been surprised by mild-mannered Oliver reacting so violently to Jock's remarks. But she was more surprised by Jock's apology, and to learn that they roomed together. And she'd expected Calvin to spar with Jock a little instead of just dummying up, and for Lucas to defend himself in some way from Jock's crude remark. Fonnie realized that she still had a lot to learn about the people here.

FONNIE KNEW SHE WOULD probably get another roommate soon. Springwillow had a waiting list and the administration wasn't going to let a bed stay empty for
long. Fonnie just wished her next roomie would be
oriented and congenial. When she met Lila Abernathy
the next morning, it took her only a few minutes to
realize that she'd been granted only half the wish. Lila
was indeed oriented, completely lucid, but she would
never in a million years win a Miss Congeniality title.

Ida Mae, long on cute but short on couth, did the introductions. "This here's Fonnie. She doesn't talk much,
but she's mighty smart. Just a little slow to get around."
Well, Fonnie thought, I've had worse intros, and then
she wondered what sweet Ida Mae would have to say
about the newest addition to Springwillow. It was worth
waiting for. "This is Lila. She says it's nobody's business how old she is, but I'm guessing her age is about
the same as her weight." Fonnie did some quick obser-
vations and concluded the magic number was somewhere between eighty-five and ninety.

"And your mouth, young lady, is as big as your shoe
size," Lila retorted. "I suggest you keep it shut except
to say 'Yes, ma'am.'"

Fonnie knew it would take more than rudeness to hush
Ida Mae. The aide ran her tongue over her bright red lips,
dropped the suitcase she was carrying, and stepped back
to the doorway. "Yes, ma'am. Would that be all, ma'am?
Or would ma'am like some help unpacking?"

"My son will unpack for me. He's in the office now signing all those blasted papers. He's probably signing my life savings away."

"Yes, ma'am," Ida Mae said. Fonnie thought she detected a slight smirk on the aide's face. Lila waved her hand in dismissal and Ida Mae skipped out the door, bouncing all the way.

Lila sat down in the straight chair by her bed and directed her attention to Fonnie. "Just so we have an understanding. I have a weak bladder and it doesn't wait well. So when I head for the bathroom you'd be wise to stay out of my way."

Fonnie was tempted to mimic Ida Mae's "Yes, ma'am" but bit her tongue instead. Since Lila was apparently waiting for a response, Fonnie finally said, "I'm sure we can come up with an equitable time-share agreement."

"And another thing—this room arrangement is only temporary. I'm first on the list for a private room when one comes available."

"That's nice," Fonnie replied. And the sooner the better, she thought. Fonnie studied the prune of a woman before her. The eighty-five or ninety years had apparently sucked all the moisture of life, as well as human kindness out of her. And the only reason Lila's still on earth, Fonnie reasoned, is because Satan is afraid she'd upset the harmony in hell.

Fonnie started to wheel herself out of the room, then

she turned back and said, "There's someone I'd like you to meet. His name is Jock Jowoski. You two should get along fabulously."

FONNIE HEADED FOR the computer room to check her e-mail. She was beginning to warm to e-mail, but it lacked a lot of being as exciting as old-fashioned snail mail. She'd loved the suspense of opening the mailbox, of taking envelopes out, of studying return addresses, of using her silver letter opener, and finally of holding the important paper in her hand. E-mail was simpler, quicker, cheaper, but it would never be as romantic.

She had two messages. The first read, *Mom, Brian coming in tomorrow. We'll see you Saturday.* Not even a "love, Amy." She knew Amy was busy with her real-estate job, but this was ridiculous. Did she communicate with her customers in that same staccato manner? Probably. After all, time is money, and an extra word means extra time. Fonnie concentrated on the message itself and tried to forget her irritation with its form. Tomorrow, she thought. That's Friday and they'll be here Saturday. Only two days away.

A sudden pain in her chest took her by surprise. It wasn't physical. It was the pain of realizing that these two people were her only living relatives. Well, there were a few cousins and a couple of nephews scattered around, but they hardly counted. Her siblings had all preceded her into eternity, as had her husband.

Brian was her only grandchild, a senior in college, and was the pride of her life. Maybe he'd marry soon, she thought, and have a houseful of kids. She would enjoy that.

Her eyes went to the second message. *Dear Gram, I'm so looking forward to seeing you. It's been a long time since Christmas. Also, I have a surprise to tell you. See you soon. Love, Brian.* Fonnie smiled in satisfaction. Now that's more like it.

She'd be glad to see both of them. It seemed much longer than four days since Amy had dumped her here. Even as the thought crossed her mind, Fonnie knew it was unfair. Amy had done no such thing. Fonnie knew she couldn't live alone and she also knew she didn't want to live with her daughter. A nursing home was the only solution, at least for now. And Fonnie had insisted on staying here in Groverton. She loved the small town snuggled in the piedmont region of North Carolina, the town where she'd lived and worked for years. She accepted the fact that Amy wouldn't be able to visit very often. Brian would be coming even less often, but Fonnie was thrilled that he chose to come now.

Calvin scooted into the computer room as Fonnie was leaving. He seemed preoccupied, and apparently didn't see her. The right front wheel of his walker brushed against Fonnie's right wheel. "Whoa there," she said, reaching out to steady his walker. "I might have to report you for DWI."

"Sorry. I guess I put my car in gear while my mind

was still in neutral." He flashed Fonnie a smile big enough for a toothpaste ad. "Forgive me?"

Fonnie smiled back. "I can forgive everything except someone ignoring me."

"Dear lady, I definitely will not ignore you. I have a little work to do here and then I would like to get acquainted with you. How about meeting me behind the rubber tree plant? I want to find out all about you."

Fonnie came out of the computer room doing her wheelie-shuffle, while at the same time her brain was making like a whirligig. Fonnie Beachum, she told herself, that man was actually flirting with you. The thought made her feel so good her wheelchair seemed to sail into the day room.

Fonnie looked around the room to decide where she wanted to park, or more exactly where she didn't want to go. Lila was standing in front of the megapuzzle, her mouth pursed as if she had just sucked on an unripe persimmon. Fonnie didn't see Jock anywhere, so that ruled out, for now, her chance to introduce the two rays of sunshine.

She saw Lucas in his usual spot, but for once, he wasn't using a magazine for a protective shield. His legs were doing an odd little jiggle that Fonnie had noticed before, and she wondered if it was a nervous twitch or if his legs pained him. She studied his face as she scooted closer. It was a kind face in spite of the deep crevices above his shaggy brows and on either cheek. His eyes squinted behind thick lenses and his mouth was a thin straight line. The few times Fonnie had noticed his face, she had seen neither a smile nor a frown. Here was a person who tried to keep his emotions to himself. Perhaps that made life simpler, she thought, or at least, easier to handle.

She headed in his direction. He must have seen her coming, because he quickly picked up a copy of *Newsweek*. He started to raise it to his eyes, then lowered it enough to watch her approach. Fonnie noticed the action and decided if she was going to talk to Lucas, she'd have to make it fast.

"Good morning, Lucas. How are you today?" She knew it was an inane question, but she had to start somewhere.

He pulled off his glasses, gave her his full attention. The thin straight line moved, the lips went neither up nor down, the words came out low and mumbled. "I'm fine. And you?"

"Good." Fonnie gave a half laugh. "Well, as good as can be expected under the circumstances."

"Circumstances?"

"Being here I mean. After all, being in a nursing home isn't usually high on anybody's wish list." Fonnie's wish right then was that the man would show some emotion, anything to prove that he was actually alive. "What do you think about it?"

His eyes held hers. His hands were motionless, his legs stopped jiggling. His mouth was still thin and straight. "I think I'm here because I need to be here. And that's fine with me. We all have a journey in life and mine led me here—as did yours."

"Yes. Of course." Fonnie was flustered. How do you

converse with someone who accepts Fate without question? Maybe a little humor would help. "On the other hand, I can think of places I'd just as soon be—a dentist's office, stranded on a desert isle."

Lucas's expression said very loudly that he was not amused. "I can't think of anyplace else I'd rather be."

That made Fonnie mad. "Then you must not have left a home you love, friends you enjoy, a family you miss."

The man in front of her twitched his mouth, swallowed hard. His voice was low and controlled. "You have no idea what I've left behind. And you never will." He carefully replaced his glasses, turned his head, and picked up the magazine.

"I'm sorry," Fonnie said. "I didn't mean to offend you." Lucas didn't respond. Fonnie tried to make the best of a bad situation. "Well, I guess my journey now is over there to put some pieces in the puzzle. Nice to talk to you."

Lucas nodded.

Actually Fonnie had no intention of going over to the puzzle as long as Lila stood there, so she was glad when she saw Calvin swivel into the room. She quickly headed for the rubber tree plant. But it seemed that she and Calvin were destined not to have a private meeting right then. The front door opened. Ginger entered followed by two men pushing a dolly. On the platform was a large wood and glass cabinet.

"That must be the aviary," Calvin said. "Let's go watch them put it up. I love to watch people work.

Brings back pleasant memories." He scooted over closer
and Fonnie followed.

"What pleasant memories? Are you perchance a
retired aviary builder?"

"No. But I am a retired contractor. I used to spend my
days just standing around watching other people work."

Fonnie smiled. "I can picture that. You probably
carried a bullwhip, and you were feared by all."

Before Calvin had a chance to respond, several others
came up to join the observers, including Jock. Gwendolyn was carrying King Tut next to her ample bosom,
stroking his head, and murmuring instructions. "Now,
Tut, when the birdies get here, you be nice and don't you
be scaring them."

"Don't pay any attention to her, Cat," Jock laughed.
"You have my permission to scare them anytime you take
a notion. I may even help you." Gwendolyn gave Jock a
look mean enough to peel paint. She clutched King Tut
tightly and flounced back to her seat in front of the TV.

Fonnie gave Jock a disapproving shake of her head,
"You ought to be ashamed of yourself, upsetting Gwendolyn like that."

Jock grinned. "Aw, she knows I was just kidding. I'm
really a very nice man."

"You could have fooled me," Calvin said. "Have you
ever tried being pleasant to anyone?"

"Yup. Tried that once. Got my face slapped. So I'm
damned if I do and I'm damned if I don't. Such is life."
Jock turned around as Oliver came up. "Just ask Oliver.

I try to be nice by arranging the magazines in alphabetical order and he gets mad as fire. Don't you, Oliver?"

"Not mad, Jock. Just aggravated at such childish behavior."

Fonnie rolled her eyes toward the ceiling. "Men!"

She turned her attention back to the workmen. They had unloaded the heavy cabinet and Ginger stood admiring it. "Isn't it beautiful?"

Fonnie had to agree. The frame was of honey oak enclosing four glass walls. She estimated it to be about four feet by three feet, and probably six feet in height. "Impressive. I didn't know aviaries came already built."

"Oh, yes," Ginger said. "And this one is top of the line: locked doors, ventilation unit, and full spectrum lighting. And notice how the perches are made to resemble real tree limbs."

"Excellent," Calvin said. "And although the birds will be completely enclosed, there are slotted openings above their perches so we can hear their songs, as well as see their beauty."

Oliver walked around the cabinet and nodded his approval. "Very good craftsmanship. When are the birds arriving? I'm really looking forward to them."

"Tomorrow. I'll put in the feed and water in the morning. And the toys."

"Toys?" Fonnie asked. "Do birds have toys?"

Ginger laughed. "You better believe it. I went wild at the pet store. I bought strings of colored blocks, a rope swing, bells they can ring, a mirror so they can preen themselves, and a multicolored bead ladder. They'll think it's Christmas." Ginger paused. "I do hope everyone enjoys them."

"Oh, they will," Fonnie reassured her. "How can anyone not like a bird?"

FONNIE NOTICED Lila had deserted the puzzle tables so Fonnie wheeled over there. Big was working on the Pinocchio puzzle, engrossed in trying to fit the puppet's red jacket together. Fonnie found a likely piece and handed it to him. Big looked up and grinned. "Thanky. Thanky. Been lookin' for that."

"You're welcome." Fonnie occupied herself a few minutes by working on the background. It seemed strange to see Big without his twin by his side. "Where's Lit this morning? I hope he's not sick."

Big glanced up from the puzzle, dropped the piece he had in his hand and searched the room. He shook his head, and Fonnie saw panic in his eyes. "Lit! Lit!" he called as he stumbled away from the card table. "Got to find Lit."

Keisha was pushing a cart of clean linen down the hall and heard Big calling for his brother. She came over and took him by the arm. "It's okay, Big," she said. "Don't worry. I'll go with you and we'll find little brother. He may have gone back to your room." Keisha folded her tiny brown hand in Big's huge white hand and together they hurried down the hall.

It wasn't long before Fonnie saw her leading them both back to the day room. The men sat down on the sofa. Keisha pulled a straight chair up in front of them, and held out a hand. "All right now, Lit, hand it over."

Lit gazed at the ceiling, a perfectly innocent look on his face. Big looked worried. "Lit, you steal again? You take candy?" Lit brought his eyes down and shrugged his shoulders. Big shook his head. "Bad. Bad boy."

Keisha smiled at the twins. "Lit isn't bad," she said. "He just forgets he's not to take candy from others. Now if you give it to me, we'll forget about it."

"Gone," Lit said, looking Keisha straight in her eyes. "It all et up."

"In that case," Keisha said, "I'll have to get the nurse to prick your finger and check your blood sugar. You might need some more insulin."

Fonnie was enjoying the exchange. She knew Keisha was trying not to laugh. At just that point Sheba jumped into the scene and blew Lit's cover story. The cat sniffed and nosed and meowed around Lit's left pant pocket. Keisha kindly asked Lit to stand and to empty his pockets. Reluctantly he complied. He hauled out a rubber band, two paper clips, a smushed cracker, a jack of hearts, and a half-eaten Milky Way.

DEACON WATCHED the scenario. When he saw the candy bar, he slowly turned and headed for his room. Once there, he jerked open the drawer of the bedside stand. One of his candy bars was gone and his paper with the incriminating drawings of fire lay open on top of his razor. That dimwit, he fumed. It wasn't enough that he stole the candy, he had to go snooping, too.

Deacon was sure that Lit wouldn't understand anything about what he'd seen, but he might blab to somebody who would understand. Somebody might actually take the fool seriously if he started talking about pictures of flames and fire. It could launch an investigation. So what was he to do?

First, he had to destroy the drawings. He tore them in tiny pieces, then slipped into the dining room where he dumped them in the garbage can to join soiled napkins and uneaten food. It'd been foolish of him to make the drawings, but he'd wanted to picture just how the flames would look. Now he'd have to be satisfied with the pictures in his head—until the real thing, of course.

He had no worry about anyone finding his contraband matches. He had them carefully hidden, just like his stock of pentobarbital, in the toe of a shoe. And he realized now that he still had a use for the sleeping potion. Instead of using it on his first intended victim, he could use the drug to get rid of Lit. It would be easy enough to lure the dolt into his room with the promise of a sweet—a poisoned candy bar. Afterwards, Lit would become sleepy, lie down for a nap, and never wake up. The perfect solution. It'd have to wait until tomorrow, though. Lit would be skittish the rest of the day after the scolding he'd gotten. But by tomorrow the fool would have forgotten all about it, and would again be craving candy.

SIX

FONNIE WOKE UP in a good mood. Her first physical therapy session was scheduled for this morning; she was eagerly looking forward to it. Keisha helped her into her pink sweat suit, and Fonnie started her wheelie-shuffle to the dining room.

But when she passed the bulletin board, her happy spirits took a nosedive. Another bold, black note warned LET HIM WHO STOLE, STEAL NO MORE. What foolishness, Fonnie thought. I hope our sneaky little writer isn't going to start listing all of mankind's possible sins one at a time. I don't know why someone hasn't spotted the culprit yet and put a stop to this nonsense.

Fonnie forgot about the foolish message when she neared the dining room and saw Ginger working on the Reality Orientation board. This was a large white board by the dining room door, called "RO" for short, which Ginger or a designee updated daily. It reminded residents of the day, month, weather, and other pertinent information. Ginger whisked away "Thursday" and replaced it with "Friday." She didn't change the weather forecast. Today would again be "sunny and breezy." Under special activities Ginger wrote, "BIRDS!"

Fonnie felt all warm inside. It was going to be a good day. She wheeled into the dining room, smiled greetings to the other early risers, and chose an empty table. She wasn't much for chatter before breakfast if she could avoid it.

Maggie spotted her from the kitchen and brought her a cup of coffee. "Black. Right?"

"Right. You remember everyone's preference?"

"I do with coffee. I've learned if they're happy with their coffee, people aren't apt to grumble so much about other things." She paused and looked at Jock at a far table. "With some exceptions."

Fonnie nodded in understanding. "If you just bring me some oatmeal, I promise not to grumble at all."

"You got it."

Breakfast here was pretty much like a short-order counter. Residents could have their choice of items as long as it didn't clash with good nutrition or a special diet. The other meals were more regimented, although the cook would consider special requests.

Maggie brought out the tray with a steaming bowl of oatmeal, a small pitcher of milk, some brown sugar, the shaker of ground cinnamon, and a slice of buttered toast. If she wasn't already feeling good, Fonnie thought, the oatmeal would have done the trick. This was the old-fashioned kind, slow-cooked with lumpy bits that rested momentarily on the tongue with texture and substance. She added just enough sugar for sweet satisfaction, but stopping short of guilt. The sprinkle of cinnamon added a bit of zest. The mixture slid down her throat with a sense of rightness. Oatmeal, she decided, should definitely be listed as soul food. She savored the last slurp, wiped her mouth, and was ready to tackle her next assignment.

Fonnie wheeled herself down the halls and smiled in anticipation when she reached the physical therapy room. Andy was waiting for her. This time he was wearing a melon-green scrub suit, tight around his biceps brachii and gluteus maximus. With such superb specimens in front of her, Fonnie had no trouble at all remembering the names of the muscles. He slicked back his already slicked-back hair and beamed at her. "Good morning, Fo-on-nie. You ready to get started?"

"Yes, sir." Suddenly her lovely day began to teeter. A cloud of self-doubt blocked out the sun of hope. "I'm a little scared though."

"Scared?"

"What if I can't do it? I'll be a prisoner in this chair for the rest of my life." Fonnie blinked hard. "Some days I think I can accept it if that happens, and on other days I think I'll go crazy."

Andy squatted down by the wheelchair so his eyes were level with hers. He reached a finger under her glasses and swiped away an escaping tear. "Fo-on-nie, you are not your body. You have a marvelous mind and a beautiful spirit. Neither can be imprisoned in a wheelchair or a bed or a nursing home. You and I will do our best to help your body, but whatever the results, your mind and spirit can soar as far and as high as you let them. Don't ever forget that."

Fonnie sniffed and nodded her head. "I'll try to remember."

The hour went quickly. Fonnie worked, pushed, pulled, sweated, prayed. At the end of her allotted time she was exhausted and hopeful. Andy was pleased.

"I've been thinking," Andy said, "that the whirlpool might be beneficial for you. Would you like to try it?"

Fonnie glanced over to the giant tub located on the opposite wall. It was enclosed on two sides, hidden from the doorway view. "A hot tub?"

"Not exactly a hot tub. We keep the water at a comfortably warm temperature. It's turned off now, but it has water jets that gently massage muscles—a form of hydrotherapy."

"You mean, I should do that instead of working with you?"

"Oh, no. I mean, in addition to our sessions. We're going to meet on Mondays, Wednesdays, and Fridays. But you could use the whirlpool on your own the other days. The warm water and the jet sprays would help your muscles relax and at the same time make them easier to move. You could get an aide to help you in and out of the tub. Twenty or thirty minutes a couple of times a week might do wonders for you."

"But I don't have a bathing suit."

"No need. Just wear some loose fitting shorts and a

light top. A T-shirt would be fine. I'll write the order if you'll give it a try. What do you say?"

"Well, sure. Why not? I can e-mail my daughter to bring me some shorts and a shirt. I could start next week." Fonnie squirmed at the thought of being seen in a wet T-shirt. It would not be a pretty sight.

When she returned to her room, Ida Mae helped her change from her sweats to a comfortable pair of gray slacks and a light sweater to match. The aide was none too gentle as she tugged the slacks up and the sweater down. "Hey, what's your hurry?" Fonnie asked. "You don't have to set a speed record getting me dressed."

"Oops. Sorry. It's just that the birds are arriving soon and I thought an old bird like you would want to be out there to greet them."

"The birds? Of course, I want to be there. What's taking you so long?"

THE AVIARY AWAITED its expected occupants. Perches and swings and branches stood ready for tiny toes to wrap around them. Seeds and suet sat in abundant supply. Residents gathered around in anticipation. Before she went out to bring in the birds, Ginger made sure that the cats were secured. Fonnie saw King Tut hiding in Gwendolyn's voluptuous lap, and Sheba purring contentedly on Lit's thighs. No problem from them.

There were four cages of birds. Fonnie noticed Oliver trying to count how many were in each cage. His head darted back and forth as the birds flapped and fluttered around. "One, two, three, four." On to the next cage, "One, two, three." Oliver shook his head. "One, two, three, four." And then the last cage, "One, two." Oliver was noticeably upset. Fonnie wanted to assure him it was all right if the cages weren't equal, that all the birds were going into the same enclosure anyway. She just hoped he didn't try to pair them up after they were in the aviary, or notice that the total number was thirteen.

Fonnie glanced around the room to gauge the reactions of the other residents. Gwendolyn was matching wits with contestants on The Price is Right, Lucas was buried in an old issue of *Life,* and Calvin was trying to maneuver his walker closer to get a better view. Jock had purposely pushed his chair back behind a Ficus plant. Keisha and Ida Mae were urging some of the other residents to watch the activities.

Ginger opened the door to the aviary, then opened the door of one of the cages. She quickly placed the cage so the two open doors connected. Then with a few snaps of her fingers, the birds left their small cage for the larger one. These were colorful parakeets. For a few moments the aviary pulsated with green, yellow, blue, and turquoise feathers. And the space reverberated with worried peeping and twittering. It didn't take long, however, for the birds to find the seeds and fruit. When the first four birds were settled either on a perch or at the feeding station, Ginger did the same thing with another cage, this one with two gray and yellow cockatiels. Their bright yellow combs pointed straight up and they looked as if they had spiked haircuts. Again a flurry of wings and feathers and then the new residents made themselves at home. Ginger picked up a third cage. This one contained four speckled cinnamon-brown finches with bright orange bills. They seemed especially nervous and jittery. It took several moments before three of them finally left the safety of their wire cage to enter the vast unknown.

Ginger's arm must have been getting tired because she let the cage slip a few inches away from the aviary door. As she did, the last of the finches flapped his wings wide, let out a high-pitched twitter and made his escape. All eyes in the room followed the tiny creature as he soared to the ceiling. Ginger hurriedly shut the aviary door, slapped her hand over her mouth, and looked bewilderingly at the escapee.

The bird swooped and glided and climbed and plummeted. It seemed to Fonnie to be an exhibition of pure joy. Tillie laughed out loud, lifted her baby doll up for a better look, and then clapped her hands. Fonnie couldn't help herself, she just had to join in the spectacle. She clapped her right hand to her left hand and tapped her right foot. Soon many of the others were clapping and shouting.

Jean ran out from the nurses' station to see what the commotion was about. Ginger ran up to her. "What am I going to do? How am I going to catch it?" The director of nursing shrugged and tried to keep from laughing.

The finch was tiring and stopped to rest a bit on the

Ficus leaves above Jock's head. Jock studied the situation a moment, rolled up his newspaper, and started to reach up to swat the bird. Fonnie cried out, "Jock. No!"

He lowered the paper and looked rather shamefaced. "I was just going to scare it away."

The bird flew up again and this time he rested on the curtain rod above one of the windows. Fonnie wheeled over to Ginger with a suggestion. "Maybe if we all leave the day room, the bird will settle down and you can coax him back into his cage."

Ginger gave her a grateful smile. "It's worth a try. I bought a small net at the pet store, but he'll have to be still long enough for me to catch him and that won't happen with all the noise."

But before Ginger could start the resident evacuation, the blob of brown took flight again, flew behind the pages of *Life,* and came to rest on Lucas's shoulder.

In less time than it took to blink her eyes, Fonnie saw the magazine drop, saw trembling hands reach up and grasp the bird. The hands then gave one twist to the fragile neck, and a lifeless body of feathers fell to the floor.

A collected gasp of horror echoed around the room. No one moved until Jean stepped into the nurses' station and grabbed some paper towels. She stalked over in front of Lucas, bent down and used the paper to pick up the headless body, and wipe up the splattered blood. Then she extended another paper towel toward Lucas. "Put it there," she demanded.

Lucas's eyes flittered from the nurse to the bloody

head in his hand. Fonnie thought he looked confused, dazed. He opened his mouth as if to say something and then closed it. He stared at Jean and the waiting towel. Very slowly Lucas brought his hand forward and deposited the decapitated head. He opened his mouth again. This time faint words came out, "But the bird shit on me."

"And for that you killed him?" Jean's voice was hard.

Lucas shook himself, like he was coming out of a stupor. He rose, brushed by Jean and several residents, and muttered, "I've got to wash my hands."

LUNCH WAS A BLEAK AFFAIR. Lucas didn't show, and several residents, including Jock, requested their trays be sent to their rooms. Even Big and Lit seemed to have lost their appetites. Calvin slid into the chair opposite Fonnie. "He didn't mean to do it, you know. A reflex action."

Fonnie wondered why Calvin felt the need to defend Lucas. How could anyone excuse what had happened? Fonnie made no comment and they ate in silence until she couldn't stand it any longer. "You may be right. It's hard to know what any of us would do under certain circumstances. I guess we'll just have to forget it."

After lunch Fonnie felt the need for a "lay down." As the old-fashioned Southern phrase passed through her mind, she wondered what had conjured up Grandma Sims and her daily afternoon nap. Fonnie clearly remembered her grandmother rising from the table and announcing, "Y'all can do the dishes. I need a lay down." At the time, young Fonnie thought taking a nap in the middle of a gorgeous day was an affront to life. She had too many splendid things to do, too much beauty to see, too many fantasies to imagine. She had no time to waste.

Now she understood. It wasn't that she was sleepy, but she had to get away—away from people, away from talk, away from life. Fortunately, Lila's son had taken her out for the afternoon, so Fonnie knew the room was hers for a while.

Fonnie caught Ida Mae's attention. The aide pushed her to the room, helped her from the wheelchair to the bed. As Ida Mae adjusted the afghan, Fonnie noticed tears in her eyes. She touched the aide's arm, and asked with concern. "What is it?"

Ida Mae sniffed and shook her head. "That was the cruellest thing I've ever seen. How could anybody kill a beautiful little bird? The bird was so lovely—so happy."

"I know. But I'm sure Lucas didn't realize what he was doing." And here I am sounding just like Calvin, trying to justify a horrendous act. "Try to put it out of your mind."

Ida Mae shook her head, "I'll never be able to forget it." She whirled and left the room.

FONNIE HAD ESCAPED from the others, but she couldn't escape her thoughts—most of them centered around Hannah. The privacy curtain was open and Fonnie gazed at the bed where Hannah had died. She remembered Hannah's twisted head, her hand caught up in the sheet, and the pillow on the bedside stand. Fonnie frowned at the last thought. What was the pillow doing there? Hannah always slept with two pillows to help her breathe better.

She tried to picture Hannah having the heart attack that was her alleged cause of death. Fonnie had seen heart attacks. The patients invariably would try to sit up, clutch the sternum area where the pain was overwhelming, and gasp for breath. If Hannah had reacted that way, she might have knocked a pillow on the floor, but surely she wouldn't have placed it on the bedside stand. And she would have cried out. Even with ear plugs, Fonnie thought, I would have heard her cry for help. And the nurses on duty would have heard something. There had been no cry.

Fonnie shook her head. Why am I bringing all this up now? Hannah's buried. Her doctor and family are satisfied. This is something I must put out of my mind. Let Hannah rest in peace.

The opening of her door interrupted Fonnie's trance. Lit shuffled in and seemed surprised to see someone in the room. Fear covered his simple face and he started to back out. "It's all right, Lit," Fonnie said. "You can come in. I don't mind."

Lit came closer. "You not mad?"

"No. I'm not mad. But I don't have any candy to give you." Lit's eyes dropped in disappointment. Fonnie scrambled around in her bedside drawer for something she could give her visitor. Her hands touched a get-well card from an old friend. She'd kept it because it was amusing. The cartoon character, an old woman, was mooning a nurse, and the caption read, "Now it's your turn." It wasn't exactly appropriate, but she doubted that Lit would understand the subtleties of the message.

"Here's a pretty card you can have." Lit reached out a pudgy hand and took the card. He smiled and nodded a thank- you, but Fonnie knew it would do nothing to satisfy his sweet tooth. She watched as he pivoted around and headed down the hall. Fonnie had no doubt he would find some chocolate covered-cherries or candy kisses to snitch somewhere. She knew she should probably alert the nurses to his pursuit, but they couldn't watch him every minute.

Fonnie had nearly an hour's rest before she heard Lila's approach. The tap, tap of her cane punctuated the tongue-lashing she was giving her son. Poor Delbert. Fonnie had only met him yesterday, but had quickly developed sympathy for him. "How many times have I've told you to count your change," Lila said. "That girl would have cheated you if I hadn't noticed it."

"Mother, it was only fifty cents."

"In my day, fifty cents was a lot of money. That's the trouble with young people today. They don't have to work for their money like I did." Delbert made no response. Fonnie chuckled to herself. Delbert could hardly be described as young. The man was at least sixty and ran his own art gallery. He certainly had no need to count change.

Fonnie rang her call bell and hoped someone would come quickly to help her out of bed. She had no hankering to spend much time with her new roommate.

Once up in her chair Fonnie went directly to the day room to see how the surviving dozen birds were doing. *We're doing very well, thank you,* the parakeet seemed to say as he swung jauntily on the blue swing. Most of the residents seemed to have gotten their fill of bird watching for the time being. Sheba prowled around the glass enclosure and from time to time would half-heartedly jump up to scare the birds, only to bump herself on the head. She soon halted this endeavor and started on her ankle massage rounds. Tillie and Gwendolyn smiled indulgently at the cat, and even Jock didn't jerk his leg away. When Sheba touched Lucas's legs, they started jiggling like puppets on a string and the cat backed away. Calvin was in the process of maneuvering his walker around the big puzzle table and Sheba's nuzzling caught him off balance. "Scat, Cat. Get out of my way or I'm liable to crush you." Sheba understood and scatted.

The cat finished his rounds of the room, but didn't stay long with any one person. She actually seemed to be searching for a particular human. Fonnie guessed that human was Lit. But Lit wasn't in the room. Big slid a rocker over next to Gwendolyn and gaped at the low-cut evening gowns on *Days of Our Lives.*

When the commercial started, Fonnie noticed that Big gazed around the room. She could tell he was looking for his little brother. Fonnie started to scoot her wheelchair past the nurses' station over to the TV.

At that moment, Ida Mae bolted into the nurses' station. She grabbed Gloria, the medication nurse, by the hand and tugged her toward the door. "You've got to look at Lit. I can't wake him up. I saw him on his bed and thought it was strange because he never takes a nap. I went in to check on him and his breathing is awful slow. Come quick."

Gloria followed Ida Mae down the hall. Big apparently heard Lit's name. He knocked over a rocking chair in his haste to get up, and scrambled to follow the nurses. Fonnie, in turn, pursued Big. Fonnie parked outside the door, but could see Gloria with her stethoscope to Lit's chest and Big patting his twin's face. "Lit sick? Lit sleep?"

Fonnie took one look at Lit's face and her nurses' instincts kicked in. Her guts told her that Lit was dying. Gloria ordered Ida Mae to get Jean and to bring a blood pressure cuff.

Jean came running up and started her examination. Temporarily forgetting she was retired, Fonnie rattled off what she thought was the diagnosis and the needed remedy. "He might be in diabetic coma. He was in my room earlier looking for candy. He must have found a treasure lode. He needs insulin."

Jean nodded, felt for a pulse, and gave instructions to Gloria. "Regular insulin, 100 units." Then she turned to the aide. "Ida Mae. Call 911 for an ambulance and bring me the portable oxygen."

Big continued to pat Lit's face until Jean gently removed his hands. She placed the oxygen mask over Lit's face, and turned back to his worried brother. "Big, we're going to help Lit get better, but he's very sick now and we have to take him to the hospital. Ida Mae will stay with you and I'll come back later and talk to you." Ida Mae gently turned Big around and led him away.

Fonnie had to squeeze her eyes shut tightly to keep back the tears. She felt in her heart that Lit was not going to make it, and his death would be tragic to his twin.

Gloria came up with the insulin syringe. "Should I check his blood sugar first?"

"No. There's not time. Give the insulin and then we'll check it." Gloria did as she was told. She had just stuck Lit's finger for the blood sugar check when the ambulance screeched to a stop at the front door. She hurriedly blotted the test tape and got out of the way as the ambulance crew lifted Lit onto the stretcher. Fonnie said a quick prayer for him as they wheeled him away.

As the front door closed behind the EMTs, Fonnie overheard Gloria give her report of the blood sugar to Jean. "This can't be right. It's 284. The insulin couldn't have worked that fast. Not if his sugar was high enough to put him in a coma."

"Well, you were in a hurry. You probably didn't get enough blood on the test strip. Don't worry about it. They'll check it in the emergency room."

Fonnie moved to the aviary. She didn't have the energy or the will to do anything. She sat and stared at the frolicking birds, and tried to put the Stanton twins out of her mind. The attempt was futile. The day room was abuzz with comments and speculations regarding Lit's collapse. And judging from the despondent faces, Fonnie knew many of residents, as well as the staff, had little hope for his recovery. After nearly an hour Fonnie started wheeling toward the nurses' station in case there was some news about Lit.

She was close enough to hear when the call came. Gloria gave out a gasp, then a low, "Oh, no."

Jean looked up from the chart she was working on, "What?"

"They couldn't save him. Lit's dead."

SADNESS SHROUDED FONNIE the rest of the afternoon. She didn't know how Jean informed Big of his brother's death, and she didn't know how Big reacted. But she could imagine. The twins had little in life, but they always had each other, and now that tie was broken. How would Big survive?

Someone besides Fonnie must have heard Gloria's report because the news of Lit's death spread around the day room, down the halls, into the craft room, into every corner of Springwillow as quickly as wildfire. Everyone loved Lit, and a black cloud of bereavement settled over the facility.

Fonnie tried to make some sense of the tragedy. Could it have been prevented? She tried to reason with herself that it was impossible for the nurses to watch

Lit's every movement. Sooner or later, he was bound to gorge himself and get sick. But who would have thought he could eat enough to go into a coma? And why hadn't the E.R. doctors been able to reverse the coma? Maybe tomorrow she'd talk to Jean about it and get more information. She'd heard the director of nursing say that she was going to work a half-day on Saturday. Yes, it would be better to wait until things settled down a little.

Fonnie sat deep in thought. She barely noticed the change of shift. The day personnel left and the afternoon staff took over. Still she sat. After a time she noticed Jock hurrying into the day room, checking his watch. She glanced at the clock on the wall—five to four. Of course, it's time for his Zoloft, and heaven help the nurse if she doesn't get it to him within the next five minutes. But the nurse spotted him also. Fonnie watched in amusement as the nurse quickly unlocked the medication room door. Jock had just gotten nicely settled when the nurse scuttled up to him and handed him a paper medicine cup. The nurse grinned and said something Fonnie couldn't hear. She couldn't hear Jock's reply, either, but she hoped it was something like "Thank you." Anyway, he would be content for the next hour or so. Right now she wouldn't have minded having an antidepressant herself. Maybe it would relieve the incessant clamor in her mind.

DEACON SMILED in satisfaction. His plan had worked. Lit had eagerly gobbled down the candy bar laced with sedative—enough sleeping medication to guarantee he would never wake up. Now that the pest was out of the way, he could concentrate on his real mission. He still favored fire as the means, but he hadn't quite worked out all the details. He would—soon.

SEVEN

FONNIE AWOKE SATURDAY morning excited about seeing Amy and Brian again. She was determined to show her daughter how well she'd adjusted to the home. She wanted both of them to be proud of her, to be pleased with her new hairdo. And she wanted absolutely no pitying glances from them. Fonnie waited until Lila left the room and then asked Keisha to help her get ready.

Keisha helped her into her lime-green pant suit, insisted she wear her gold chains, applied a little blush to her cheeks and dabbed her with Gardenia cologne.

"Now hold your head up high, Fonnie, and smile like you have a wad of money hidden in your bra. That's what I do when I go out, and it drives the boys crazy."

Fonnie laughed until tears came into her eyes. "I'm not going out, Keisha, and I'm not trying to impress any boys."

"Don't be so sure about that. There's two boys in the lobby right now who'll go ga-ga over you. Of course, Mr. Jowoski won't let it show, but I assure you Calvin will be tripping over his walker to get close."

Fonnie sat up straight in her chair, lifted her head, and pushed out her chest. "Well, let's go see. But before we do, I need to talk to Jean. Could you help me find her?"

"She was in her office a few minutes ago working on the time sheet. I'll push you down."

Jean looked up, but kept her pencil poised over a grid of Xs and Os. Fonnie knew making out a work schedule for the nursing staff was more challenging and frustrating than the Sunday crossword puzzle. "I hate to interrupt, but I wanted to ask you something."

"Of course," Jean smiled, and let the pencil drop. She twirled her chair around so the desk was no longer between them. Jean wore a light-weight, short sleeve, pant uniform with white socks and Keds. Fonnie had seen a myriad of changes in nursing through the years, many of which made her cringe, but she thoroughly approved of the relaxed dress code. Gone were the stiffly starched white dress uniforms and the white hose that had to be handwashed. Gone, also, were the perky caps anchored to the top of their heads with invisible bobby pins. Her white cap with the black ribbon across the top made a lovely graduation portrait, but it was only in the way when trying to work. Now health professionals wore anything that was practical and comfortable, and it was fine with Fonnie.

Jean looked at her visitor and arched her eyebrows. "So, what can I do for you?"

"About Lit. What did the doctor say was the cause of death?"

"What do you mean?" Jean's voice held surprise and irritation. "You said yourself it was diabetic coma."

"I know. But that was because I'd seen him scrounging around for candy. What if it was something else?"

"What makes you think now it was something else?"

"I overheard Gloria telling you his blood sugar was only 284. That's not high enough to precipitate a coma." Fonnie felt Jean was becoming annoyed, but it couldn't be helped. There was something peculiar about the situation. And Fonnie didn't like peculiar.

"Then you also overheard what I told Gloria, that she probably hadn't gotten enough blood on the test strip."

"Yes, but…."

"And remember that Gloria had already given Lit regular insulin, which you know is fast-acting."

"Not *that* fast acting." Fonnie refused to be pushed into accepting an explanation that wasn't credible. "What was his blood sugar in the E.R.?"

"I don't know. We haven't received the E.R. report yet or the death certificate. The hospital will send them over in a few days. In the meantime, I suggest you not worry about it."

"In the meantime, Lit will be buried and it'll be too late for an autopsy."

"An autopsy? Really, Fonnie, there's no reason to have an autopsy. Besides, the state won't pay for one unless it's ordered by the police. And the police aren't involved in this."

"Of course." Fonnie wheeled around, afraid if she stayed any longer she'd say something she might regret. Jean was a good nurse, usually very reasonable, but in this case she was being closed-minded. Or, Fonnie pondered, am I just being foolish? Maybe the stroke did affect my mind, as well as my body. She'd known stroke victims who had become paranoid, suspicious. Was it happening to her? She longed for someone she could confide in, someone who would respect her thoughts and opinions, and yet be honest with her.

As Fonnie did her wheelie-shuffle into the day room, she wondered if she could talk to anyone there about her suspicions. There were only a few residents that Fonnie considered cognizant enough to even discuss the situation. Could she entrust her misgivings to Gwendolyn or Maude or Calvin or Jock? Would any of them hear her out, or would they brush her off as Jean had done?

As Fonnie was contemplating her possible confidants, Hannah's frightened voice echoed in her brain. "I saw Deacon. He's here. He's evil."

With a start, Fonnie realized for the first time, that if Deacon really existed he could be one of the men sitting in the day room at that very moment. He could be a man she'd talked to, laughed with, sat beside in the dining room—a friend. That meant she had to keep her suspicions to herself. If she talked to the wrong person, she could be putting herself in danger.

Fonnie glanced at the bulletin board. The bold message from yesterday that warned those who stole to steal no more was gone. Could it have been a warning—a warning to Lit? But Lit couldn't read, and had only the vaguest idea of what stealing meant. Had Deacon posted the warning? And then made sure that Lit would steal no more? Did Springwillow have a murderer among its residents?

Fonnie had to find time to digest these new thoughts and feelings. Avoiding the other residents, she wheeled over to where Big was sitting by himself in a corner. She reached out and patted his hand, not knowing what to say. He looked up. He smiled. "Lit is with Papa and Mama. Jean told me. They'll take care of him now."

Bless Jean, Fonnie thought. She'd said exactly the right thing. "That's right, Big. You took care of him while he was here, and now they will do it."

Sheba pussyfooted over to them, mewing forlornly. "She misses Lit," Fonnie said. "Do you want to hold her?"

Big shook his head slowly, his eyes wary. "No. You take her."

Fonnie reached down with her good hand and scooped up the yellowish ball of fur. She stroked the cat's back until Sheba succumbed to the friendly fingers, closed her eyes and snoozed. Fonnie closed her own eyes also, but her brain couldn't rest. She couldn't accept Lit's departure from this world as easily as Big and Sheba had. Fonnie swore to herself that Lit's demise would not be blindly written off as a natural death, as Hannah's had. She planned to do some investigating of her own.

AFTER LUNCH, Fonnie assumed a position in front of the Ficus plant where she was out of the line of traffic, but had a clear view of the front door. There was a steady stream of visitors, and each time the door opened, Fonnie looked up expectantly. She spotted Brian first as he pulled open the heavy door, then stepped back so his mother could enter.

Such a handsome boy—young man—Fonnie corrected herself. He had Harrison's thick, dark blond hair and his ready smile. But where his grandfather had been rather short and stocky, Brian was lean, lanky, gangling. His limbs seemed to have outgrown his frame. Even when he was comfortably seated, his legs and arms kept searching for places to rest.

Brian let the door slam shut behind him as he spied his grandmother. He rushed up and buzzed her cheek. "Hey, Gram. Mom said you had your hair cut, but she didn't tell me you were lit up like a firecracker."

Fonnie patted her hair. "Like it?"

"Love it. Doesn't she look great, Mom?"

Amy hesitated. "Yes. It's very nice. It's—flattering—makes you look younger." Amy bent down and kissed her mother.

Fonnie smiled. Amy was a lousy liar, but at least she tried. Fonnie was proud of her daughter even though their personalities sometimes clashed. Fonnie thought Amy was too uptight, too much business and not enough fun. Even today, when she could have dressed in causal jeans, Amy had on a beige linen skirt and a matching pointelle sweater, with a single strand of pearls. Her reddish-blond hair was cut in a short bob and her makeup was flawless. And Fonnie knew Amy considered her mother too unconventional, too casual. But Fonnie wanted their visit today to be without any controversy. "Pull up some chairs and tell me about life on the outside."

"Gram, you sound like you've been doing hard time." Brian scooted a chair closer and his voice lowered. "Has it been so bad?"

"No. No, of course not." Fonnie shook her head. "I didn't mean to come across like a whiner. It's a lovely place, nice nurses, lots of activities, and I've made some friends. I'm really very happy here."

"I'm so glad you've adjusted, Mom," Amy said. "You had me a bit worried at first."

"No need for you to worry. I'm doing great." Unlike her daughter, Fonnie had always been a good liar, and today she was outdoing herself.

"Well," Brian said, as he got up and started pushing the wheelchair, "it's a fantastic day outside and we're going out to get some fresh air. Then you can tell me what you've been up to besides getting your hair frizzed."

"Good idea," Amy said. "Brian, you push her out on the patio while I get her a sweater from her room. The wind is still a little cool." Amy shifted a plastic bag under her arm. "I found a pair of shorts and a T-shirt you wanted, but they're so old and dingy, I wish you'd let me buy you some new ones."

"No. No, they'll do fine. It's not like I'm going to be on a public beach." Fonnie's face lit up at the thought of beaches and water and swimming. "Although I wish I could go to a beach. I used to love swimming. It was the one sport I was good at."

"Yeah. I remember when you and Gramp took me once on a church picnic. You were splashing around in the water, swimming circles around us kids. All the other old women were sitting in the shade yelling at us to be careful."

"What do you mean, 'other old women?' I wasn't an old woman at the time."

Brian grinned. "No, you weren't. And you're still not. Now point me in the direction of the patio. Let's get outside for a few minutes."

When they came to the patio door, Fonnie gave Brian instructions in proper wheelchair exiting. "It's easier if you turn the chair around and back me out while you hold the door open with one foot."

Brian did as he was told, but complained about the procedure. "Why don't they install a button you can just push to open the door? That way you could come out by yourself."

"Yes, but some of the residents would be continually pushing the button just to see the door open. I guess it's a judgement call between convenience and practicality."

Fonnie breathed deeply of the spring air. A Chinese wind chime tinkled gently in the cool breeze. The wind caressed her cheeks and played tag with her hair. It reminded her of long walks and a gentle hand to hold. Here on the patio she could almost forget that she was no longer able to take long walks, or any other kinds of walks. She was surrounded by kindness, but she still felt like a prisoner—a prisoner of her own body.

Brian surveyed the patio area, enclosed on three sides by wings of the building and on the fourth by a low brick wall. "Hey, this is nice. Pansies, daffodils. What's that yellow bush?"

"Forsythia. Isn't it blooming beautifully? I guess because it's so sheltered. And before long there'll be tulips. And Ginger tells me they'll be setting out petunias, marigolds, and heliotrope soon. It's very lovely." But not as lovely as my yard at home, she added to herself.

"Look, Gram, up there under the eaves. Some kind of bird building a nest. And there's a bird feeder. I love to watch birds flitting in and out at a feeder. Yes, indeed, very nice."

Amy joined them, slipped a sweater around her mother's shoulders, and sat down on the edge of the bench facing her. "I hate to bring it up, Mom, but we do need to discuss your house. The market is good now. I don't think I'd have any problem selling it. I know how you feel about giving up your home, but…"

"You have no idea how I feel about giving up my home." Fonnie's voice was sharper than she intended it to be. "You came here expecting me to give you an argument about selling. You thought I would cry and carry on. Well, you should know by now I'm not a wimp. Of course we'll put the house on the market and it'll sell quickly and some other family will make a wonderful life there. I miss it and I will continue to miss it, but I'll not whimper about it."

Amy leaned back with a look of satisfaction. "Then that's settled. I'm glad you're being so sensible." Her voice caught a little as she went on, "You know, it's hard on me, too. It's the home I grew up in. And where you helped me get back on my feet after the divorce. I'll miss it, too."

"Of course you will." Fonnie gave her daughter a reassuring smile, "I didn't mean to be snippy. I assume you and Brian are staying there this weekend while you're visiting me?"

Amy nodded. Brian dragged a yard chair closer, its metal legs grating on the cement. "And Gram, I went rummaging this morning in the hall closet. I had no idea you'd saved all the toys I had when we lived with you— the windup train that went around in circles, the bulldozer I used in the sandpile. The toolbox, by the way, was missing a saw. Wonder what happened to that?"

"Your saw went in the trash can when your grandfather caught you trying to saw the legs off a chair. It was only my deft intervention that saved the rest of the tools."

"Well, I do thank you. And if it's all right with you, I'm going to confiscate everything in the closet. I may have a little devil of my own some day who would enjoy hammering on furniture."

Fonnie's mind immediately pictured a room full of little devils all looking exactly like Brian. "I'm glad you want the toys. I never could bear to give them to Goodwill. And I want you to go through the house and take anything you like. You, too, Amy. Whatever is left you can donate to some charity. Except my unicorn collection," she added hastily. "I haven't decided what to do about that." She smiled at both of them. "And don't worry about me. I'll still have my home—in my memory.

"Now let's move on to something else. Brian, you said you had a surprise for me. And since I don't see a gift, it must be something to tell me. So—out with it."

Brian bobbed his head up and down. "Yes. I have something to tell you."

He gulped a couple of times. Fonnie assumed he was trying to find the right words. "Well, go on," she encouraged him.

"You know, I've changed majors a couple of times in college." This time Fonnie bobbed her head and waited for what was to come. "Well, I know what I want to do with my life now." He rubbed a big hand across his chin, and glanced at his mother. Amy's eyes were fixed on her feet. "Gram, I'm going to be a cop!" His grin rivaled that of a circus clown. "Oops!" Brian slapped his face. "I'm supposed to say 'law enforcement officer.'" His face sobered but his eyes still grinned. "I'm going to have a career in law enforcement."

"Is that right?" Fonnie said. She tried to hide the excitement that started to bubble up in her brain. Imagine-a cop in my own family. Now maybe I'll have someone I could talk to about my suspicions. However, the look on Amy's face made her realize she had to tread lightly. "It sounds interesting."

"No it doesn't! The whole idea is ludicrous." Amy

spat out the words. "I've tried to tell him it's a complete waste of his education. It's a dangerous job and the pay's pitiful." Amy gave her mother an imploring look. "Tell him, Mom. Tell him he can't make a decent living being a policeman."

Fonnie's attention went from Amy to Brian. Amy smoldered in anger. Brian sparkled with delight. It was no contest. But before Fonnie could state her opinion, Brian turned to his mother. "Mom, I want a career that will give me a life—not just a living. And I'm not going to settle for anything less." Brian reached out and took one of Amy's hands. "Tell me the truth. Are you happy working in real estate? When you wake up in the morning are you eager to face the day, go to the office, call your clients, show the houses?"

"That has nothing to do with it. I have a good job. It pays well. It's a good living." She pulled her hand out of his grasp, scooted back on the bench. "And may I remind you that my job has supported us very nicely ever since your father walked out."

"I understand that. But that's not what I asked. Are you happy in your job?"

Amy shook her head. "That's not the point."

"Yes, Mom, that is the point. I need to do something that I'm happy doing. And I need a job that gives me more than a paycheck." Brian turned to Fonnie. "Gram, were you happy being a nurse?"

Fonnie thought about the question. "I never really considered it that way. I would describe it more as being content or feeling fulfilled. When I entered nursing school, I wasn't sure it would be right for me. But I soon realized I was doing what I was meant to do with my life. You might say I found my destiny. A person can't ask for anything more than that."

"I might know you'd side with him," Amy lashed out. "Neither one of you has any common sense."

"I'm not siding with him. I just meant to point out that if he's drawn to law enforcement then he should give it a try. He'll find out soon enough if it's right."

"Sure—well, we can discuss it later." Amy stood up, smoothed her skirt, straightened her sweater. "I think it's time to be going. I've got some business to take care of this afternoon. Ready, Brian?"

Fonnie reached her hand out and touched Brian's arm as he started to get up. "Why don't you run along, Amy?" Fonnie gave her daughter an innocent smile. "I'd like Brian to stay awhile and talk. Couldn't you come back for him later?"

"Oh, he can stay as long as he likes. He insisted we drive both cars." Amy bent down to kiss her mother. "I'll be back tomorrow and we can talk more then. I really have to make some business calls now."

After Amy left, Fonnie and Brian sat in silence, absorbing the afternoon sun, each apparently lost in private thoughts. Fonnie broke the stillness. "It's so peaceful out here. It's hard to believe that evil resides within those walls."

Brian scowled. "Evil? What are you talking about?"

"I need your help, Brian. That's why I'm glad your mother had to leave. If she heard what I'm going to tell you, she'd just say I was getting dotty."

"Tell me what?"

Fonnie looked earnestly at her grandson. "If you really want to be a cop, you can start right now."

DEACON SAT AND STARED into space. He looked like he was about to fall asleep, but looks could be deceiving. His mind was speeding faster than a runaway race horse. He was detailing his plan of destruction, but he dared not put any of it down on paper. No telling who else might be snooping around. He had nearly all of it mapped out in his brain.

He had to disengage the smoke detectors, and shut off the water supply to the sprinklers. He knew how to do both. He'd learned about electrical wiring and the fundamentals of plumbing. Now he could put that knowledge to use.

First the smoke alarms. That wouldn't be hard to do. He knew where the maintenance room was which held all the electrical wires, the incoming water pipes. Of course the room was off-limits to residents, but that wouldn't stop him. Doors that residents were not supposed to enter had rough pieces of tape scrolled around the knob. The theory being that if a resident accidently started to open the door, he or she would feel the tape and abruptly turn around. Yeah, right.

Actually, the door should have been kept locked, but

Jimmy, the maintenance man, seldom bothered. Jimmy also hadn't bothered to fix the door scraping against the floor. Deacon had entered the room to study the wires and pipes. He hadn't been noticed, but the noise the scraping door made worried him. He located the breaker box, and noted the wires that he needed to cut. He didn't have any wire cutters, but he'd confiscated a sharp pair of scissors from the craft room. He reckoned that scissors used to cut tongue blades and twistums could cut electrical wire. He had only to snip the ground wire or the neutral wire and the smoke detectors would not activate. They were supposed to have battery backups, but Jimmy was careless, and Deacon doubted that the batteries were ever checked.

Next would be the sprinkler system. The water to the sprinklers wasn't hooked into the domestic line. They had their own water supply. All he had to do was turn off the valve at the stand pipe. The sprinkler sensors would still react to the rising heat, the sensors would melt as they were intended to do, but there would be no water behind them to come gushing out.

Yes, an admirable plan. Now to decide where to start the fire. And make dead sure of his own escape route.

EIGHT

BRIAN STUDIED HIS grandmother, concern evident in his eyes. "What do you mean I can start being a cop now?"

"It's a long story, but hear me out." Fonnie looked up as a visitor pushed another wheelchair out on the patio. She made sure they were out of earshot before proceeding. "There have been two unexpected and suspicious deaths here within the last few days. I didn't think too much about the first one until I remembered the pillow on the bedside stand. But I'm sure the second one is the result of foul play."

"Whoa there. Are you saying patients have been murdered here?"

"Yes. Only they're called residents, not patients."

"I don't care what they're called. I want to know why you're making such an outrageous charge?"

Fonnie sighed. "That's what I'm trying to tell you. Let me start at the beginning. You have a notebook?"

"Notebook?" Brian patted his jacket pockets, brought out a couple of envelopes and a stubby pencil. "Okay, the detective is ready. Fire away."

Fonnie fired. She told him of Hannah's fear of a man called Deacon, that she'd said he was evil, and that she'd died the same night. "At first I accepted the explanation of a heart attack, but when I remembered the pillow, it made me wonder."

Brian stopped his scribbling to ask, "The pillow?"

"It was on her bedside stand—like it had been placed there, not tossed or accidently pushed. And I realized Hannah wouldn't have done that. She needed two pillows to sleep on, to breathe easier." Fonnie paused. She wanted to remember all the details so Brian could get the complete picture. "And her hand was tangled in the sheet as if she had been thrashing about."

Brian shook his head, his stare uncomprehending.

"Don't you see? Maybe she was struggling with someone."

"So what do you think happened?"

"She was smothered. Someone snuck in, or is it sneaked? Anyway, someone came into the room, probably covered her mouth so she couldn't scream out, pulled a pillow out from under her head and smothered her with it. She tried to struggle, but he was strong, too strong for her. She couldn't move, she couldn't breathe. And she couldn't cry out because the pillow was held too tightly over her face. Then when the monster was finished, he lifted the pillow off and instead of replacing it under her head, he put it on the bedside stand. Maybe he actually wanted to leave a clue, wanted someone to guess that it wasn't a natural death." Fonnie shifted her weight in the wheelchair and watched Brian's reaction. "What do you think?"

Brian scrunched up his face. "I don't know. Sounds mighty thin to me."

"But the plot thickens. Let's go on to the second one."

Again Fonnie tried to start at the beginning, about Lit being a diabetic, about him wandering around in search of something to satisfy his sweet tooth, about him coming into her room yesterday hoping to find some candy. "He didn't find any in my room, but he must have somewhere else. A few hours later he was unconscious and died in the emergency room. But I'm not sure he died from his diabetes." Fonnie reached out and snatched Brian's hand as a sudden thought came to her. "The warnings. I didn't tell you about the warnings."

"Warnings?"

"Signs on the bulletin board. It's only for official notices, but someone has posted different warnings. They're printed in big black letters."

"What did they say?"

"The first one read, 'I am Alpha and Omega.'"

Brian nodded. "It's Greek, means beginning and ending. Not very original."

"Of course it's not original. It's from the Bible—the book of The Revelation to be exact."

"I know that, Gram. What I meant was that the phrase has been bandied around so much, it's lost its impact. It's used in crossword puzzles, even in advertising. I don't know how you can construe it as a warning."

"Actually I didn't. But the second one was more menacing. It was from Romans. 'Vengeance is mine, I will repay.' But it wasn't until the third notice was posted, and after Lit died, that I recognized them as warnings."

"And the third one was what?" Fonnie could tell Brian was getting impatient, but she was talking as fast as she could.

"It read, 'Let him who stole, steal no more.' It's from the book of Ephesians."

"Boy," Brian looked with admiration at his grandmother. "You sure know your Bible."

"Not necessarily. I looked them up in my concordance. But that's beside the point. Don't you see? It was a warning. Lit was stealing and someone killed him to put a stop to it."

"Gram, really. No one is going to kill a person for snitching a little candy."

"But suppose Lit stole more than candy. Suppose while he was snooping around he found something valuable and took it. Or broke it. And whomever it belonged to decided to get revenge."

"Instead of just reporting it? That's crazy."

"Exactly. We're talking about a mentally ill person who killed Hannah because she remembered him and killed Lit because he stole something."

"I don't know, Gram. It's all pretty iffy. You have no proof that the deaths weren't natural. And even if they weren't, there's no reason for you to become involved. You simply need to tell your suspicions to someone in authority and leave it up to them."

"I tried that. I talked to Jean, the director of nursing,

but she brushed me off. And the administrator doesn't work on weekends—not that he would take me seriously." Fonnie gave Brian a dejected look. "But I thought you would believe me."

"It's not that I don't believe you. It's just that it might be dangerous. And it's not really your job."

"Not my job? That's exactly what I tried to tell myself when I first became suspicious. That's the same thing people have said for eons to escape their responsibilities, to soothe their consciences." Fonnie sat up straighter in her wheelchair, held her shoulders back. "But I can't hide behind that delusion. I have to do what I can to ferret out the truth. Some people may say that the lives of Hannah and Lit weren't valuable, that their deaths were unimportant. But no life and no death are unimportant. It *is* my job to find out what really happened, since no one else will do it."

Brian gave an apologetic shrug. "I guess it wouldn't hurt to look into things some more. Are we going to do some snooping or should we call the police?"

"No police yet." A dark cloud scuttled in front of the afternoon sun. Fonnie shivered and pulled her sweater tighter over her arms. "I thought before we talk to anyone else, you could help me get some information on the suspects."

"You have suspects?"

"At least four. They're probably all in the day room right now. Would you like me to introduce you to them?"

"And you'd say what? 'This is my grandson and he's

going to be a cop and he's investigating some murders here and would you please tell him where you were when the victims died?' I'm sure that would go over big."

Fonnie gave him a tolerant smile. "I'm sure we could be a little more subtle than that. You could say, 'I'm doing a term paper for a psychology class on how the male ego adjusts to an environment that is mostly female-dominated.' Most nursing homes are, you know—in both staff and residents. Although, you may not notice it here since most of the women tend to hang out in the craft room. But how does that line sound?"

"Fishy. And it wouldn't get me any needed information. Just tell me who these suspects are, what you know about them and why you suspect them."

"Well, actually I don't really suspect them at all. They're all very nice people, I'm sure. It's just that they fit the profile. That is, they're male. Hannah specifically said, 'he' and 'him.' They're able to walk and write and think, so it's possible one of them could have done it. You still have enough paper for your notes?"

Brian split open the envelope he was writing on to make more room for his detective work. "So who are these suspects and what do you know about them?"

"All right, here they are—in no particular order. Calvin Flynt. I haven't gotten to know him very well yet. He's charming, intelligent, retired from the construction business. He uses a walker, but he can maneuver it around with great dexterity. He spends a lot of time in the computer room. He told me once he was checking on his stocks, so he must be heavily invested. Oh, and he's traveled a lot, at least around the South because he was talking about hotels in Atlanta and Savannah. That's about all I know."

"Married? Family? Visitors?"

"He hasn't had any visitors that I've seen since I've been here, and we haven't really had personal conversations so I don't know about his family."

"Okay. Next."

"Lucas Parker. Very quiet, stays to himself, reads *National Geographic*. Sits with Tillie during meals and reminds her to eat. Tillie is definitely spaced out and Lucas seems to have taken a special interest in her. He's rather aloof to everyone else. And he believes in Fate."

"What do you mean, he believes in Fate?"

"He told me that Fate brought him here. I don't exactly understand what he meant by that. It could go back to the old theological question. Do we have free will to make decisions, or are we puppets in the hands of a whimsical God?"

Brian shook his head, "Let's not go there. We do enough of that in the dorm." He scribbled some more and then lifted his pencil and his eyes, indicating that he was ready to continue.

"Oh, and he killed a bird."

"Who killed a bird?"

"Lucas. A finch escaped from the aviary and happened to land on his arm. Lucas reached up and decapitated the poor thing."

"Good God. That's terrible. He must have a violent temper."

"Not really. The bird just surprised him. He said it messed on his shirt and he lashed back without thinking. It's not like he planned it." Fonnie paused and then added, "But speaking of tempers. Oliver Jefferson has one. He almost came to blows at the bingo game because of some teasing."

Brian scribbled down the name. "I take it he's one of the suspects."

"Yes. He acts crazy at times, but I wonder if it could be just an act."

"Oh? Sounds interesting. Tell me more."

"He's obsessive about geometric neatness. Or, at least, pretends to be. He likes everything lined up in order—magazines according to size, napkin holders in the exact center of the table, chairs lined up correctly. He'll go into the dining room after every meal and place each chair in precisely the right place. I watched him yesterday. Each chair has to be the same distance from the table and from each other. He places three chairs at each table and leaves the fourth place empty for a wheelchair. Except where the Four Musketeers sit." Brian opened his mouth, but before he could ask the question, Fonnie explained. "The Four Musketeers are four very nice ladies who always sit together, and Oliver makes sure their table has four chairs. And, let me see," Fonnie paused, trying to get her thoughts together, "when he works on a puzzle, he gets very upset if somebody puts in an inside piece before all the outside frame is completed."

"Would he be crazy enough to kill somebody because they upset his idea of a geometric universe?"

"Perhaps. If Lit had moved something out of order in his room." Fonnie was getting tired and wanted nothing more than to go to her room and rest, but she had to tell Brian everything while she had the chance. "The other possible suspect is Jock Jowoski. He sounds mean enough to kill somebody, but I think it's all bark and no bite. He's a retired lawyer. He takes antidepressants during the day and sleeping pills at night. He denies having known Hannah before he came here."

"You asked him that?"

"It came up. I wasn't grilling him." Fonnie sighed. "Not much there really. But I don't think any of the other male residents have the capacity to murder."

"And you're convinced the culprit is a resident? Why not a staff member? You do have male nurses or therapists or orderlies, don't you?"

"Yes, but Hannah was killed during the night, and…" Fonnie's voice trailed off.

"And what?"

"It's just that I feel that it must be someone our age, someone old. I figured Hannah had recognized someone she'd known when she was young, which would now make him old. Does that make sense?"

Brian gave her a half smile. "I guess so. But it seems to me what we need to do first is to find out just what killed Lit. How can we get our hands on the emergency room record? Can't you get the administrator to call the hospital and have it sent over?"

"It's the weekend, remember? The charge nurse on duty today could call, but I doubt if she'd do it on my say-so. She'll wonder what the hurry was since the hospital routinely sends over reports when they get around to it."

Brian slid his pencil behind his right ear until only the rubber eraser remained in sight. He gazed at the lengthening shadows, apparently deep in thought. After a few moments, he looked back at his grandmother, "Would his regular doctor here be the same one who treated him in the hospital?"

"Probably not. The hospital has resident physicians who cover the emergency room. Why do you ask?"

"I could call the E.R. I have my cell phone. I could say I'm doctor so-and-so's assistant and that I'm trying to catch up on paperwork this weekend and I need a copy of the record and that I'll be over in a few minutes to pick it up. How does that sound?"

Fonnie beamed at the new detective in the family. "Sounds good to me. His doctor is Floyd Nettleton. I saw him when he came in to check on the twins. I don't know if he has a PA or not. Maybe you could say you're his new office assistant. It might just work. Hospitals are chronically understaffed on weekends. No one is going to take the time to check on your story."

"And if it doesn't work out, we won't be any worse off. I mean, we can't be prosecuted for giving false identification. Can we?"

IT WORKED. Brian returned in less than an hour. He'd made the call as planned, then drove to the hospital and was given a copy of the report. No questions asked. He hurried back to Springwillow. It was nearing suppertime. Fonnie was anxiously waiting for him in the day room. She instructed him to push her behind the aviary where they would have more privacy. Fonnie barely noticed the snatches of song and chattering coming from the birds. She was only intent on the paper in Brian's hand.

Brian pulled up the rocking chair, and handed the report to his grandmother. "I tried to read it, but the handwriting is atrocious, and that medical jargon doesn't mean much to me. What do you make of it?"

Fonnie scanned the record. "It's pretty simple." She pointed a carefully trimmed fingernail at the history section. "This is information called by our nurse. It gives Lit's diagnosis as IDDM. That means insulin dependent diabetes mellitus. He was found unconscious, unable to arouse. Allegedly ate large amount candy/carbo. Given 100 units of regular insulin." Fonnie shifted her finger to the next section and read aloud. "'Presenting condition—unresponsive, cyanotic, constricted pupils. Physical exam—lungs clear, abdomen soft, respirations—6, pulse—140, blood pressure—70/30, blood sugar—200.'" Fonnie shook her head.

"Looks like he was in pretty bad shape."

"Yes," Fonnie agreed. Her finger slid down to the treatment section. "Airway established and oxygen en route to hospital. The treatment in the hospital consisted of IV Normal Saline, IV insulin, IV antibiotic, and IV stimulants."

Brian frowned. "Why antibiotics?"

"To cover all the bases. Diabetic coma most often occurs when there's an underlying infection. Although Lit certainly didn't seem to be coming down with any illness. And it happened so quickly." Fonnie paused. "Something's not right."

Brian now pointed to the bottom section of the E.R. sheet. "What's this scribbling?"

"That says there was no response to treatment. The cause of death is given as irreversible diabetic coma."

"So, I don't see anything suspicious. The doctor didn't question the cause of death. He didn't order any other lab tests. He apparently didn't think there was any reason for an autopsy." He studied his grandmother for her reaction. "What do you think?"

Suddenly, Fonnie felt very, very tired. "I can't think anymore right now, Brian. Maybe I've been wrong about everything. Will you push me to my room? I'll have supper there. I don't feel up to talking to anyone."

Deacon was worried. Was that aide, Ida Mae, suspicious of him? It seemed to him she was acting funny. She'd shied away from him this morning when she was making his bed, hurried through her tasks without saying a word. Like she could hardly wait to get out of his room.

Did she see Lit in my room yesterday? Or maybe she saw Lit leaving my room licking chocolate off his lips? Or, even worse, maybe Lit said something to her before he lapsed into unconsciousness.

He'd have to keep an eye on that girl. Perhaps talk to her to find out what, if anything, she knew. There was no way some silly girl was going to mess up his plans now.

NINE

BRIAN PHONED HIS mother, told her he was going to stay and have supper with Gram. Brian sat deep in thought while Fonnie picked at her broiled chicken and baked potato. He'd refused the offer of a tray for himself. "I'll stop and get a Big Mac when I leave here. You eat while I think." He glanced at the door. "How much time do we have alone?"

"At least an hour. Lila watches the national news in the lobby after supper."

"Good. I have no desire to meet your roommate from Hell tonight."

Fonnie shook her head. "I did not call her that. I just said she was a cross between Cinderella's stepmother and the Grinch. I don't know how you got the idea she was unpleasant."

Brian gave a deep, throaty laugh. "Gram, you're impossible. But let's forget her and get back to the case. That is, if you think we still have one. I'm about ready to pack it in."

"No, we can't quit now. We still have a case. I admit that E.R. report almost convinced me otherwise, but

I've been thinking about that." Fonnie took a big bite of her brownie. "Lit, no doubt, had a DNR order."

"DNR?"

"Do Not Resuscitate. It's an advance directive. Most people sign one when they enter a nursing home. I know I did. In Lit's case, his relatives probably signed it. It means that if we stop breathing, the staff is supposed to allow us to die without attempting extraordinary means to bring us back to life."

"Sounds morbid to me."

"Not at all. Just realistic. At any rate, if Lit had one, it would have been sent with him to the hospital. Therefore, the E.R. staff did what they could to reverse what they were told was a diabetic coma. When that failed, they didn't attempt to put him on life support. And the doctor didn't order any other tests because he assumed his condition was caused by his diabetes."

"But if it wasn't his diabetes, what could it have been?"

"Poison. Or some kind of overdose. Many things could have caused the coma. But the E.R. staff didn't look for any other causative agent. And I guess we can't blame them, given Lit's history. Now the only way to find out is an autopsy. And the chance of getting an order for one is pretty slim. So where do we go from here? Any ideas?"

"You mean, besides quitting?"

"Brian, you know me better than that. I'm not a quitter. Now stop talking nonsense and put your cop hat back on."

"Okay, okay. Let's talk about your suspects. You said

earlier that one reason you thought the culprit was a resident is because Hannah died, or was killed, during the night. But of course, there's staff here at night."

"Of course. However, not the same staff. That is, most of the staff members work the same shift most of the time. A few of them rotate shifts, but most pick the shift they like and stick to it. So if Hannah saw Deacon during the day and if he was a staff person, then it's unlikely he'd be working that night."

"Yeah, I guess you're right. But if a resident was wandering around at night, surely a nurse or an aide would see him."

"Not necessarily. There's a skeleton crew on at night. If they were busy, which they always are, someone could easily sneak from one room to another without being noticed."

"All right. Then how about the sneaker's roommate? Wouldn't the other person in the room hear him getting up and going out and wonder about it? Maybe we need to interview all the suspects' roommates."

"I've thought about that. Wouldn't do any good."

"Why?"

"Calvin has a private room. Which is another reason why I think he must make good money in the stock market. Private rooms are expensive here. Lucas's roommate is completely nonresponsive. I don't know his medical history, but I know the man doesn't talk or move. It's possible he may hear, but if he did, he probably couldn't process the information, and he definitely couldn't tell anybody about it. The other two are roommates, themselves."

"So Jock and Oliver share a room. Wouldn't one tell on the other—if there was anything to tell?"

"I'm sure they would if they knew anything. But Oliver wears a hearing aid, which he removes at night, so it would take an earthquake to wake him. And Jock takes a sleeping pill, so it'd probably take two earthquakes to wake him up." A frown crossed Fonnie's brow. "Of course, if Jock wanted to be awake, he could refuse his sleeping pill."

Brian cradled his chin in his hands as he contemplated his grandmother. "Who do you want it to be?"

Tears glistened in Fonnie's eyes. "I don't want it to be any of them."

FONNIE AWOKE TO the sound of rain sluicing across her window. She reached over and pulled up the blinds to better watch the downpour. The weather mirrored her emotions. She was in a storm of denial and self-doubt. She wondered if any of the suspicions she'd confided to Brian yesterday had validity. Both deaths could have been natural. And if so, then all of her so-called suspects were innocent. That was what she wanted to believe. And for nearly an hour she did.

During that hour, Carlotta had gotten Fonnie up and dressed before Lila stirred. But when the aide wheeled Fonnie out of the bathroom, her roommate was awake and bitching. Lila started a tirade against the rain, against her bladder condition, and against folks who hogged the facilities. "You, of all people, Fonnie, should know that the blasted rain only intensifies the strain on my weak bladder. But what are you doing? Lollygagging in the bathroom as if you were the only person in the world that has to use the throne."

Fonnie raised her eyebrows. "Excuse me, Lila. I could do my business in the bed, but then you'd only complain about the smell. It's what's known as a lose-lose proposition."

Carlotta smothered a smile and pushed Fonnie out the door. Fonnie leaned back and fired a parting shot, "I'll see your sunny face at breakfast. I hear we're having fried tripe."

FONNIE LIKED TO vary her seat at meals for a change of view and a change of company. This morning she slid her chair next to Gwendolyn. Gwendolyn enjoyed talking when she wasn't watching TV. She greeted Fonnie with a grin and waggled all three chins. "Lovely day for ducks. Wouldn't you say?"

"Looks like. At least we don't have to worry about getting out in it. You expecting any visitors today?" Fonnie really wasn't interested, but felt she had to make small talk.

"Maybe so. It's too wet for my son to play golf, so he may drop in. Of course, I know my daughter won't make it. The damp weather is hard on her arthritis. She really needs a hip replacement, but the doctor says she has to lose fifty pounds before he'll do it." Gwendolyn sighed. "Not much chance of that. She has low metabolism like I do. We only have to look at food and we gain weight."

Fonnie nodded, but she noticed that Gwendolyn was doing a lot more than just looking at food. She chomped her second piece of toast that had been slathered with butter and strawberry jelly, and washed it down with coffee steeped in sugar.

The other residents who regularly ate in the dining room straggled in one by one. Fonnie smiled at each of them in turn. How could she ever have suspected shy Lucas, grumpy Jock, handsome Calvin, or obsessive Oliver of anything evil? She'd have to call Brian and tell him to forget all her foolish ideas.

After breakfast, Fonnie did her wheelie-shuffle into the day room. She felt mellow. It was going to be a good day. But her day was shattered as she rolled by the bulletin board. There in front of her eyes was another warning! THERE WENT OUT FIRE FROM THE LORD AND DEVOURED THEM. Fonnie began to shake; her hands trembled; her heart raced. When she gained control of herself, she hurried to the nurses' station. "I need to use the phone. I must call my grandson."

Gloria looked surprised, but didn't question her. "Sure. Want me to dial for you?"

"Please." Fonnie rattled off Brian's cell phone number and then took the phone.

It rang four times before a sleepy voice answered, "Yeah?"

"Can you come right away? I need to talk to you."

"Gram? Are you all right?"

"Just come."

"Sure. Be right there."

AFTER HER PHONE CALL, Fonnie looked around the day room. It was nearly empty. None of the usual men were sitting around. She saw a few residents heading for the Chapel for the nine-o'clock service. The local churches took turns conducting the Sunday morning worship service. In years past she'd been among the choir members of her church who came to participate. She had enjoyed it then, and under different circumstances, she would probably have enjoyed going now. But today she had other things on her mind.

An elderly gentleman approached the nurses' station. "I'm Harold Stanton's cousin," he said to Gloria. "I've come to take him to Howard's funeral. And I'm going to keep him at my house for the night."

Gloria nodded, handed him a pen, showed him the sign-out book. "We're all going to miss Lit. He was a joy to have around." The gentleman smiled a thank-you.

Lousy weather for a funeral, Fonnie thought. Or was it? Maybe it was fitting for the heavens to cry over the death of an innocent soul.

Lila plopped down beside Gwendolyn in front of the TV. Robert Schuller reminded them that miracles can indeed happen. King Tut was ensconced somewhere in Gwendolyn's skirts and Sheba was nudging Lila's arm. Lila kept her eyes on the screen as she reached down and started petting the cat. That was miracle enough for Fonnie. Lila may not have an ounce of kindness for humans, but apparently she did for animals. Go figure.

Fonnie decided to wait for Brian in her room and told Gloria to send him down when he arrived. While she waited, Fonnie reached for her King James Bible, flipped to the concordance, and soon located the warning verse. It was in the tenth chapter of Leviticus: *And there went out fire from the Lord, and devoured them, and they died before the Lord.* The context of the verse made it clear that God destroyed two men because they had burned incense that God had not commanded. Fonnie frowned. She doubted that incense burning was a common practice at Springwillow. So what was going on in our writer's twisted mind?

Brian came in shaking his head and shaking the rain off his Braves' cap. "Okay, Gram, what's so important you had to mess with my Sunday morning snooze?"

"There's been another warning." Fonnie gripped Brian's hand. "I'm really scared. We've got to stop him. We've got to stop this crazed person. It has to be the man Hannah called 'Deacon' and we must find out who he is and stop him."

Brian sat on the bed and listened intently as his

grandmother told him of the message on the bulletin board, the verse in the Bible, and of her fear that the evil Deacon intended to destroy Springwillow by fire. He patted her hand and gently released her hold on him. He rose, walked to the window, and stared at the rain for several moments. He cleared his throat and looked back at her. "I know that you think this Deacon is real, that he's evil, that's he's already killed two people, and that now he plans to kill others. But, Gram, I don't believe it. I thought about it a lot last night after I left here. There's nothing there. You can't put any credence in posted Bible verses. They're all over the place. Driving over here I saw a sign next to the ABC store that read, 'Prepare to meet thy God.' Does that mean that everyone who goes in to buy a bottle of liquor is going to be shot by a hidden sniper?"

He came back and stood in front of her wheelchair. Fonnie gazed at the middle of his pullover until she slowly lifted her face to meet his eyes. Her mind slid back a mere dozen years to when he had to raise his eyes to meet hers. Back to a time when he believed everything she told him. Now he was saying he didn't believe her. It was no use. If Brian didn't believe her, then nobody would.

"So I'm just to let the whole thing drop?"

"Yes."

"And you won't play detective with me any longer?"

"No." Brian put his hands on his hips and licked his lips.

Fonnie figured he was trying to get up courage to say something else, so she helped him out. "And?"

"And I'm fixing to leave for Myrtle Beach. Some buddies of mine are waiting for me."

"But your mother said you were spending your spring break with us."

"I know. But she misunderstood. You know Mom. She twists things the way she wants them. I told her I was going to spend a couple of days with her and coming to see you. That's all. I'm sorry. I really have to go."

Fonnie smiled. "Of course you do. I hope the rain stops soon so you can enjoy the rest of your break." Fonnie knew she was lying when she said the words. She didn't hope the rain would stop. She hoped Myrtle Beach would be washed out to the middle of the Atlantic, and that Brian and all his spring-break buddies would be stranded with no sun, no girls and no beer. It'd serve him right!

Brian gave a sigh of relief. "Thanks, Gram. I knew you'd understand. The rain is already letting up. Supposed to stop by noon. It's going to be a beautiful afternoon." He gave her a buss on the cheek. "I'll e-mail you when I get back to school."

Fonnie watched her detective skip out the door. *So it's all up to me now.*

THE LAUNDRY ROOM would be the ideal place to start the fire. Deacon had decided that early on. And now would be a good time to check it out. Deacon ignored the rough tape on the door handle that was meant to deter his entry. The washers and dryers sat empty. The shelves were stacked with clean sheets, towels, washcloths. The tables where linen was folded were bare. No one worked in the laundry on Sundays, but the door wasn't locked so the aides could get in if they needed extra sheets or whatever.

Deacon studied the layout. It would be easy enough to torch a pile of linen. He would rip some towels in smaller pieces and use them for kindling—like starting a bonfire. He'd start the fire under one of the wooden tables. Before long, it, too, would catch fire and there would be a roaring blaze. The flames and especially the smoke would slither down the hall, creep into every room, and choke out his enemies. He no longer named them individually. All the residents were his enemies. He couldn't articulate why exactly, but he knew they were.

Of course, he'd planned his own escape. The doors leading outside from the residents' area weren't locked because of safety codes. But they were equipped with alarms which alerted the nurses when a door was opened in case some resident became confused and accidently wandered out. Deacon wasn't about to announce his leaving with a clanging alarm. He would leave by the employee's door. This door was located at the rear of the building. It was the one door that was kept locked and didn't have an alarm. It was opened by the employee entering a secret code into a push-button keypad. Secret? Huh! It had taken him less than twenty minutes one afternoon to learn the combination. He had stationed himself in a shadowed doorway by the exit when the day shift staff started to leave. They were chatting, fumbling for their car keys and punching in the code with no thought of secrecy.

One thing he hadn't decided yet was what to do afterwards. He wanted to hang around long enough to see the devastation, to watch the fire trucks that would eventually arrive, to revel in all the excitement. He might let himself back in by the staff entrance, if that part of the building wasn't destroyed. Then he could see first hand the destructive force of vengeance. Or he might just slip away into the night. He had some money hidden away, other identities he could try on. He'd figure that out later. Right now he had to decide just when to implement his plan.

It had to be soon. He'd already given the warning—not that anyone ever took his warnings seriously. If this blasted rain would stop, he'd do it tonight.

Deacon slipped out of the laundry room at the same moment that Ida Mae came waltzing down the hall. She was humming and happy. That changed immediately. "What were you doing in there?" Her voice was sharp, her eyes leery.

"I…I was looking for Keisha. I thought I saw her coming this way. She, ah-h, forgot to leave me a clean towel this morning." Deacon dropped his eyes. "I'll find her later."

"Never mind. I'll get your towel. Keisha's busy on the other end of the hall." Ida Mae stepped around him, opened the door, grabbed a towel off the shelf, and shoved it at him. "Anything else?"

Deacon lightly brushed her hand as he took the towel. She snatched back as if she'd been burned. He gave her a half-smile. "What's the matter, Ida Mae? Don't you like me?"

She backed away and didn't answer the question. "Just stay out of places where you don't belong." She turned and hurried down the hall. This time she wasn't dancing.

TEN

FONNIE WAITED NEARLY an hour after Brian left before venturing out of her room. She used the hour to make plans. If Brian really thought she was going to drop her investigation, he didn't know his grandmother very well. Nothing was going to stop her. First she was going to take the message off the bulletin board, if it hadn't already been snatched off and tossed away. She intended to keep it and turn it over to the police later for fingerprints. In the meantime she had to interview each suspect until she had enough information to implicate one of them. Then she would insist that the police be called. The problem? She knew her time was limited. Could she find out Deacon's identity before he struck again? There was no doubt in her mind now that Deacon was real and that he was evil. And that she had to find out who he was.

A sudden gust of wind rattled the window by her bed. It also rattled her nerves. For the first time Fonnie realized that what she was doing was risky. Brian had mentioned danger when he tried to convince her that finding the murderer wasn't her job. At the time, she'd ignored the idea, but now she had to admit it was a very real possibility. When she first read the warning about a devouring fire, she'd been scared for the nursing home, the residents, the staff. Now she was scared for herself.

Deacon had killed two people. He would not hesitate to kill again. She shuddered when she remembered there had been only a thin privacy curtain between them the night he smothered poor Hannah. What would prevent him from coming around the curtain the next time? Fonnie knew right then that she would not be wearing her ear plugs again, indeed she may not even sleep again until the villain was revealed.

Fonnie inhaled deeply as she'd been taught in a long-ago meditation class, but the time for meditating was over. Now was a time for action—no matter what the danger. She wheeled herself as quickly as possible to the day room.

She was pleased to see that Calvin was alone in front of the big puzzle. He seemed deep in thought, and Fonnie wondered if the puzzle was really what had him in such a trancelike state. Before heading in that direction, though, she picked up a copy of *Good Housekeeping,* scuffled toward the bulletin board, removed the warning, and slid it between the pages of the magazine.

Then she wheeled over to the puzzle. "Looks like Mount Kilimanjaro is nearly completed. A good puzzle worker like you should be able to finish it in a breeze."

"Huh?" Calvin lifted his head and stared at Fonnie for a second or two. Then he bestowed a dazzling smile on her. "Oh, sure, especially now that I have you here to help."

"I don't think I'd be much help. The rain seems to have made me restless. Somehow, it brings back memories of being young and foolish. Remember when a spring rain was an excuse to go barefoot through mud puddles? To squish mud between your toes, and then wash your feet off under the drain gutter?"

Calvin laughed. "I can't say I have those kinds of memories. My grandmother would have thrashed me if I'd played in the rain."

"You lived with your grandmother?"

"Yes."

"Around here?"

Calvin nodded. "A little farm out in the country." His eyes seemed to glaze over as past years slipped by. "It was all right if I worked in the rain. But not played." He shook himself and came back to the present. "What about you? Did you grow up here?"

"No. In the eastern part of the state. But my husband and I lived here all of our married life."

"Just the opposite with me. I took off as soon as I could, started traveling and never stopped, even when my wife and kid left. She said I loved my job more than them. I guess she was right. She remarried. He's in Dallas. We don't communicate much."

Fonnie was touched by the loneliness in his voice. Even though she and Amy had their differences, they knew they could always depend on each other. Suddenly

Fonnie felt ashamed of herself. She had no right to dredge up a friend's painful memories just because of her silly suspicions.

But her suspicions weren't silly, Fonnie reminded herself. She had to keep on. "I'm surprised that you came back here, then, to enter Springwillow. Do you know someone in the facility, or have friends in the area?"

Calvin shook his head. "No. It just seemed like as good a place as any."

"Homing instinct, maybe?" Fonnie wasn't sure this conversation was going anywhere. She just couldn't think of the right questions to ask.

"Maybe. Like Robert Louis Stevenson said, 'to behold again in dying, the hills of home.'"

Calvin gave a quick laugh. "Not that I'm dying. My doctor says my ticker is as wobbly as my legs, but I don't quite believe that. Anyway, I like it here. The ladies are charming and the nurses are pretty. What more could I ask?"

Fonnie wished she could think of something more to ask, but her mind came up dry. Then she remembered the beauty shop gossip. She didn't for a minute think Calvin spent his computer time pouring over porn, but what actually did he do? "I notice you enjoy computers. Working on some project?"

"Not exactly. I check my stocks quite often. And then I like to piddle around on different web sites. It's amazing what you can find. After Ginger brought the birds in, I wondered why she hadn't gotten any canaries.

So I got online and did some investigating, and I found out that canaries don't do well in the same cage with parakeets. Interesting, huh?"

"Very interesting." Fonnie was impressed. She had only recently been initiated to computers and knew she had a lot more to learn. "Oh, by the way, I nearly forgot, but I was asked to give you a message by one of our charming ladies."

Calvin's eyes popped wide. "And what message would that be?"

"Maude says they need a man's help in the craft room. I can't imagine what for. Perhaps to open those pesky little paint jars."

"Or to keep their knitting yarn from getting tangled. I used to do that for my grandmother. I might just go down and lend the ladies a hand some day." Calvin grinned. "But not right now. I think I hear a computer calling me."

With Calvin gone, Fonnie looked around for another interrogatee. She saw Lucas come in and head for his favorite chair. As she wheeled over, Fonnie fished in her head for a good friendly opener, hoping he'd forgotten their last unfortunate conversation. She came out with, "I've been watching you in the dining room and I think it is so nice the way you help Tillie. You're a very thoughtful person."

Lucas looked surprised, as if he was not accustomed to compliments, then shrugged. "She's sick. Sick people need help." He scowled. "They shouldn't be put down or laughed at. Sick people should be helped."

"Of course, and I admire you for doing it. Did you happen to know Tillie before you came here? I take it you are from this area."

Lucas shook his head. "No. That is, yes, I lived here when I was younger, but I didn't know Tillie. My work took me away for years."

"I think it's so interesting to know what kind of work people did before retirement. I was a nurse, a registered nurse. What was your line?"

Lucas leaned back in his chair, his legs began to jiggle. "Many things. I tried many things. Insurance, mostly. I sold insurance." He reached for a magazine and started flipping the pages.

Fonnie recognized that the conversation was over. She smiled. "Nice chatting with you. I think I'll go see what Gwendolyn is watching." *Insurance salesman, my foot,* Fonnie thought. That man couldn't sell a homeowner's policy to a man whose house was burning down.

Jock was standing by the aviary watching its occupants flit around. Fonnie scooted over to him. "And you tried to make everyone believe you didn't like birds. Here you are enjoying them just like the rest of us."

He grinned. "Not enjoying. Wondering."

"Wondering what?"

"Why Ginger got all male parakeets."

"How on earth can you tell they're males? I would think *that* knowledge was confined to God and other parakeets."

"And to someone who used to breed them for a

hobby. You can tell their sex by the color of the skin at the nostrils, just above the bill. In the male the color is purplish-blue, while in the female it's brownish. These are all males."

"Sounds like I'm talking to the Birdman of Alcatraz. When does an attorney find time to raise birds?"

Jock's grin vanished. "Even attorneys have downtime." He turned as if to leave, Fonnie grasped for something to say. "If you want to discuss strange hobbies, I can top that. I collected unicorns."

That stopped Jock in his tracks. "An educated, professional woman collected mythical animals?"

"Sure. Figurines, paintings, drawings, references in literature. It's amazing how popular the magical creatures are. They're even mentioned three times in the Bible."

"Ah, but only in the King James version. The other translations say 'wild oxen.'"

Fonnie caught her breath. "I didn't know you were such a biblical scholar."

"Just part of being a Renaissance man."

The ringing of a faint bell brought people to their feet and started wheelchairs wheeling. Jock motioned for Fonnie to go ahead of him. "Lunch awaits, madam."

Fonnie preceded him into the dining room. She saw Oliver sitting alone and wheeled to his table. She noticed Jock hesitate, then join them. Fonnie thought it rather strange, that for roommates, they spent very little time together outside of their room. Apparently they had little in common, and didn't enjoy each other's company. At this point, Fonnie wasn't concerned with their uneasiness. She had to complete one more interview.

Oliver looked up from rearranging the plastic flowers on the table. To Fonnie's surprise, it was Oliver who started his own interrogation. "Was that your daughter visiting yesterday, Fonnie?"

Fonnie beamed. "Yes. She's in real estate, does very well."

"I'm sure you're proud of her."

"Of course. Just like any mother would be." And like any mother, Fonnie thought, she loved to talk about her family, but this wasn't getting her the information she needed. It was time to turn the conversation around. "And I'm sure your mother was proud of you becoming a teacher. You must not have taught here though, or you would have had my daughter as a student. Where did you teach?"

Oliver took both hands and brushed back the sides of his hair. He seemed to be considering his answer as silence hovered over the table. Finally he said very slowly, "She might have been proud. I don't really know. She died when I was young."

"I'm sorry. I didn't know." Fonnie was flustered.

Jock came to her rescue. "Of course she would be proud. Working your way through college—Chapel Hill, wasn't it? That's a tough school to get into, let alone get through."

Both Oliver and Fonnie gave Jock a grateful smile. "Yes," Oliver said, "you're right. And she'd be proud of my thirty-year career." He then evidently recalled Fonnie's question about where he had taught. "In Wilkes County, lovely area, nice people. I intended to stay there, was on a waiting list at a nursing home there for a bed, but my heart condition worsened, and my doctor got me in here."

"Well, this is close enough for family and friends to visit you," Fonnie reassured him.

"I don't have any close family, but some of my friends have come down, even some former students."

Jock propped his chin in his left hand and gave Oliver a mischievous grin. *Uh-oh,* Fonnie thought, *Jock has been nice for just about as long as he can stand.* His next words proved she was right. "Those students probably came down to check and see if you still know how to count."

Oliver gave his roommate a half-smile. "I'll forget how to breathe before I forget how to count."

After lunch, Fonnie waited in the day room for Amy's arrival. It was still raining, although it seemed to have let up a bit. As she waited, Fonnie recalled Oliver's words about being proud of her daughter. *But have I told her that lately? Probably not. I've been too concerned with my own situation. But Amy needs to know that I'm proud of how she's made a life as a single mom, as a professional person, of how she's handled my affairs.*

So when Amy came through the big double doors, shook the rain off her umbrella, and strolled over to meet her mother, Fonnie scrunched up as far as she could in her chair, reached up her right arm and greeted her daughter with a hug.

Amy bent down, squeezed her mother's neck. "You must know I stopped by the deli on my way in and brought you those eclairs you like so much."

"You brought me exactly what I wanted—you."

DEACON WATCHED FONNIE. She worried him. Was there something fishy about the way she'd questioned him. Could she be suspicious? She'd been Hannah's roommate. Could she have possibly seen him there that night? No. Impossible. She'd been sound asleep. Or was she?

It was bad enough having Ida Mae look at him like he was a bogeyman without this busybody nosing around. He'd have to do something about both of them.

The girl had to be first. There was no doubt about that. She'd be off duty at three this afternoon. Heavens knows who she might talk to about what she'd seen, or thought she'd seen. He couldn't take that chance.

Deacon moved slowly toward the chapel. He had a plan.

ELEVEN

AFTER AMY LEFT, Fonnie felt the need to be alone with her thoughts. She hadn't shared her suspicions with Amy. She had to sort them out in her own mind one more time, and then decide how to proceed.

Lila had informed her earlier that Delbert was taking her out to a concert at their church this afternoon. Her voice oozed through transparent lips. "Too bad your daughter won't take you out any."

"My daughter has more sense than to take me out in this kind of weather." Then Fonnie couldn't resist adding, "Besides I'm blacklisted in every church in town— ever since the news leaked out that I'm a practicing witch." Lila's eyes and mouth both flew so wide open her cheeks completely disappeared. Fonnie did a quick wheelie and scooted away before her roomie could recover. Let her chew on that little tidbit, Fonnie thought. She'll think twice before she orders me out of the bathroom again.

Fonnie waited until Lila and Delbert left the premises before she asked Keisha to help her to her room. "I hope you don't mind. Ida Mae is my assigned aide today, but I don't see her around."

"I don't mind, Fonnie. But I'm a little worried about Ida Mae. She just doesn't seem to be herself lately. It's probably that blasted diet she's on."

"Diet? Why should she be on a diet?"

"She thinks she's getting fat. Sure, she might have a few extra pounds, but she looks fine to me. Besides, no one can have the strength to do this job if you don't eat right. She was so weak this morning she had to call me to help get Gwendolyn out of the tub."

Keisha got Fonnie settled on her bed and started to put the wheelchair in the corner. The aide picked up *Good Housekeeping* from the seat. "I'll take this back out to the day room."

"No." Fonnie grabbed for the magazine. "I was saving that to finish reading an article. Just give it to me."

Keisha tossed the magazine on the bed. The piece of paper with bold letters slipped part way out. Fonnie quickly covered it with her afghan. "Thanks. I'll be fine now."

After Keisha left the room, Fonnie studied the message again. THERE WENT OUT FIRE FROM THE LORD AND DEVOURED THEM. Maybe Brian was right. Messages like these are common: painted on rough boards, posted on telephone poles, plastered over cracked windows. Fonnie even remembered on the way to Springwillow she'd seen a sign on an empty building which read, "Don't lie to God." She'd never paid any attention to the signs before. Why was she taking this so seriously? Call it a gut feeling. And in her gut, she knew there had been two murders already here and others were planned.

She shook her head, dug in the bedside drawer for a notebook and pencil. *It's time to get down to business,* she thought. She divided a page into four columns. She headed each column with a name: Jock—Oliver—Lucas—Calvin. Under each name Fonnie wrote anything she knew that could connect her suspects to either the Bible messages, to Hannah's or Lit's deaths or any suspicious actions on their part.

Jock: Bible scholar, lived in same area as Hannah—may have possibly known her, could have hoarded his sleeping pills and used them to overdose Lit, hates cats. (How can anyone hate cats?)

Oliver: Wilkes County—close to where Hannah grew up, quoted a Bible verse, obsessive about symmetry/neatness. (Does he have other obsessions?)

Lucas: seems secretive, lied about his occupation (I think), has a nervous twitch. (Could this be indicative of a mental problem?) Killed a bird.

Calvin: traveled a lot so may have met Hannah, private room so could write messages without being seen, apparently has money (did he get it honestly?)

On the bottom of the page Fonnie wrote, *All of them: strong enough to smother Hannah, seem sane but a lot of insane people do, had equal opportunity to perform the vile acts.*

Then Fonnie thought about Hannah's statement, "His name didn't fit." Why would she say that? Fonnie went through the suspects again. Jock: an obvious nick-name—what is his real name? Oliver: an old fashioned name. Does it have significance? Lucas: was that Latin for 'light'? Calvin: was he named for John Calvin, the reformer? Really nothing there.

Fonnie had to admit she had precious little evidence to accuse anyone of a crime. If only Brian hadn't left. He might have been able to find further information. Again she hoped it was raining as hard at the beach as it was here.

DEACON SLIPPED INTO the hush of the chapel. Recessed lights behind the altar illuminated a stained-glass pastoral scene of lambs and leopards and cows and bears all lying peacefully together in a field of wildflow-ers. He took little notice of the ambience: the dark wooden walls, the thick wine-colored carpet, the set of four pews on either side of the center aisle, the kneeling rail awaiting those who sought either solace or forgive-ness; he was too busy planning his strategy.

The chapel was a perfect setting, not only because he would get rid of an obstruction to his divine plan, but also because the room was isolated and seldom used. The only services scheduled were Sunday morning and Wednesday evening. The rest of the time it was open for those residents who wanted to drop in for prayer or re-flection. Few did.

First Deacon went to the side of the altar and pushed a button on the CD player. Soft organ music flowed out, music meant to soothe a troubled soul, calm an anxious spirit. It wasn't loud enough to muffle a scream, but then Deacon didn't plan to give his prey a chance to scream. He fondled the plastic cord in his pocket. He'd cut it from a roll in the craft room with the scissors he'd already stolen. He didn't know what its original intended use was, but it was ideal for his need.

Next he rehearsed the upcoming drama. He knew exactly how he was going to lure Ida Mae into the room. There were two call bells in the chapel: one by the door and one by the kneeling rail. Springwillow residents were never far from a bell if they needed to call for help. And he knew whichever aide was closest was supposed to respond to that call. Deacon had it all worked out. All he had to do now was wait.

Deacon waited just inside the chapel door. He left the door open wide enough so he could see anyone coming down the hall, but no one could see him. It was nearing three o'clock. The aides would be making their last rounds before clocking out for the day. He'd learned their routine well. Each aide was to check her assigned rooms to be sure things were in order—no lunch trays forgotten, no immediate needs of the residents. These rounds were cursory at best as the aides were all anxious to get through and get out. This was Ida Mae's assigned hall. He knew she wouldn't routinely check the chapel, but she would have to respond if a call bell lit up above the door.

He waited until she came out of the next room, then flipped on the call bell, hurried toward the altar, hunched down on the far right of the front pew. The lights were dim, the organ music played sweetly in the background. Deacon's head was bowed as if in prayer.

Ida Mae opened the door. A shaft of bright light skidded down the middle aisle. The rest of the room remained in shadows. "Hey, who's here? Need some help?"

Before Ida Mae came any further, Deacon reached for the call bell near the railing and turned it off. He didn't want anyone else coming in. Then he resumed his position and moaned, followed by a raspy cry. "Pain. Chest pain." He kept his voice low and guttural so the aide would have to come closer to hear. She did.

Deacon lifted his eyes enough so he could watch her bounce down the aisle and slip into the pew with him. He repeated his groan, clenched his hands to his chest.

"You're having chest pain?" She started to slide back. "I'll get a nurse to help."

"No." Deacon sat straight up. "Don't leave me."

Ida Mae flinched, recoiled against the back of the pew, inhaled deeply. "What do you want?"

Good. She recognized him. Deacon smiled as his right hand reached into his pocket. He wanted her to know him, to know that she couldn't stop him, to know he would have his revenge. "I want you to help me." His left hand touched her trembling arm. "I want you to like me."

She raised both hands in front of her face. Even in the dim light, he could see terror in her eyes. "Get away from me. Don't touch me."

She swung her legs to the left, turned her back to him,

tried to stand up. The plastic cord slipped easily around her throat, encircled her pretty neck, then tightened with a quick jerk. Her intended scream ended in a whimper. She flailed one hand behind her head trying to get to him while the other hand pulled at the cord, trying to loosen its hold. He sneered at her pitiful efforts. Her legs kicked several times against the front of the pew. Soon their movements were reduced to occasional twitches. He was a little disappointed that she hadn't struggled more.

At the end, her head dropped backward against his chest. He studied her face for several moments: her blond bangs tangled in the frames of her glasses, her chubby cheeks with splotches of red rouge, her lips turning a bluish hue.

Deacon let the cord slip off, coiled it carefully and replaced it in his pocket. He slid back and let Ida Mae's head sink onto the cushioned pew.

TWELVE

THE AFTERNOON SHIFT came on. Fonnie got back up into her wheelchair. She avoided the day room. She didn't feel up to conversing with anybody. On her way to the computer room to check her e-mail, Fonnie saw Sheba wandering down the hall. The cat was nosing into doors, sniffing around potted plants, mewing her loneliness. Fonnie scooped Sheba up onto her lap. "I know you miss Lit. But you can be my special friend, if you like. I need a friend right now." Fonnie continued shuffling her chair down the hall and continued talking to the cat. "I'm scared, Sheba, really scared. Something bad is going to happen and I have to stop it. But I'm not sure that I can."

Sheba's response to Fonnie's confession was to burrow deeper into her lap and to lick the dangling fingers of her left hand. Fonnie halted the wheelchair, reached over with her right hand, and stroked the cat's soft fur. This elicited soothing murmurs that sounded almost like a gentle breeze. Fonnie breathed deeply of the peaceful moment, and felt her mind and her muscles relax.

She hadn't realized she'd been so uptight. She slowed her breathing to correspond with Sheba's intermittent purrs. It was in between breaths and purrs, that another sound filtered into Fonnie's brain. A step? A door opening? Fonnie twisted around in her chair. The hallway behind her was empty. Most of the doors stood open, but no one was in sight. *There I go again,* she thought, *getting spooked over nothing.*

Fonnie hurried on to the computer room. It was empty also. She pulled up to the closest monitor. She didn't really expect any e-mail. Amy had probably just gotten home and Brian was, no doubt, playing volleyball on the beach. But she wanted to check it anyway. She was pleasantly surprised.

Dear Gram,
Weatherman wrong. Still raining here. Instead of playing on the beach, my buddies (Frank and Ben) and I are playing with your mystery. I told them all about it and they think you may be right. Ben e-mailed his dad who is a lawyer in Asheville. His dad knows of Jowoski, says he dropped out of sight several years ago—didn't retire, just quit. He's going to try to find out more. Could Jowoski be hiding a deep, dark secret? About Oliver—if you let me know where he taught, we might be able to learn something. Frank is a computer nut. He can find out things like what the governor eats for breakfast (he prefers hash-browns to grits. Can you believe that?).

Let me know if there's anything else we can do.
Love, Brian

Fonnie beamed. So Brian hadn't deserted her after all. She began to feel a glimmer of hope. She didn't understand the ins and outs of the Internet, but maybe Frank could dig up some information that would help. She wasted no time in writing back.

Dear Brian,
Bless you and Ben and Frank. And bless the rain. Ask Frank to find out anything he can on all four suspects. You never know what might pop up.
Oliver retired from Wilkes County schools. I don't know how that will help us, but you might be able to find out if he had any mental problems while there.
And what is Jock Jowoski's real first name? That might prove helpful to know.
Calvin was raised in this area, but traveled a lot. Maybe you can get a line on that.
Lucas told me he was an insurance salesman, but I don't believe him.
Just let me know anything you find out. I'll check with you again after supper.

Fonnie tried to think if there was anything else she should say when a shadow covered the screen. She glanced over her right shoulder straight into Calvin's smiling eyes.

"Oh, I didn't hear you come in."

"Good. I just finished oiling the wheels on my walker.

They were beginning to squeak a little, but I've fixed that. Now I can go anywhere without announcing my presence in advance."

Fonnie squirmed in her chair. "That's nice," she said. "There's nothing as irritating as a squeaking wheel." She continued to crane her neck at him. She wished he would move on, away from her back. She became very uncomfortable with him standing there. Was he trying to read what she had written? And that faint noise she'd heard in the hallway-could that have been him? His room was on this hall. Perhaps he was coming out and had heard her words to Sheba. Would the words have any meaning to him?

Fonnie felt a chill starting at the base of her spine. She swung around to the keyboard, grabbed the mouse, quickly clicked on Send. Her e-mail message disappeared. But had it been soon enough? And why didn't Calvin move? She didn't look around, but she sensed he was leaning closer. Was Deacon about to be revealed?

To keep her right hand from shaking, Fonnie clutched the arm of her wheelchair. She was afraid to say anything for fear that her voice would shake also. She had to think. She had to think fast. The call bell was less than four feet away, but it could have been a mile away for all the good it was. Calvin and a blasted Ficus plant stood between her and the bell.

A door slammed in the hallway. The sound brought her back to her senses. She was within screaming distance of help. No need to panic. Apparently the sound was also an incentive for Calvin to propel his newly oiled wheels to the other side of the room.

"Guess I'll check and see how Mobil Oil is doing. You never can tell how some stocks will do. Up one week and down the next."

Fonnie nodded. She couldn't care less about oil or any other stocks. She just wanted to get out of there. "I think I'll check on the birds," she finally managed to say.

Calvin smiled. "I'll see you later."

Sheba had slept peaceably in Fonnie's lap throughout the entire scary episode. "Fine friend you are," Fonnie whispered as she wheeled out of the room. She needed time to think, but Fonnie didn't want to be alone in her room. She decided she would indeed check on the birds. Behind the aviary was a good place to sit and think, and still be in sight of others.

DEACON WASN'T CONCERNED about Ida Mae's body being found anytime soon. She might be reported missing by a distraught mother or roommate or boyfriend, but they would think she'd disappeared after she left Springwillow. Sooner or later someone would notice her car in the employee parking lot, but it really wouldn't matter. Ida Mae was history. When or how she was found didn't interest him.

He had other things to think about now. The rain was letting up again and he hoped it would clear by nightfall. He had to ready his plan. Deacon finished his supper and knew this would be the best time to make final preparations. Most of the residents were either engrossed in the evening news or resting in their rooms. The nurses were preparing the evening medications and the aides were busy with the late feeders.

He surveyed the hallway leading to the maintenance room that contained the electrical and mechanical equipment. It was located at the end of hall D along with the physical therapy room, the craft room, and the admitting office. No one would be in any of those rooms on Sunday evening. The hall lights were turned off except for one bulb above the door marked as an emergency exit.

The door to the maintenance room was not locked. Deacon's hand caressed the rough tape on the door handle. The tape was to remind residents the room was off-limits. Deacon smiled at the thought. Much of his life has been spent going places and doing things that were off-limits. He opened the door and slid in. The door scraping across the floor was louder than before. Deacon shook his head. Jimmy was a lousy maintenance man. If this place wasn't about to be burned down, Deacon would have reported Jimmy's sorry ass.

But he couldn't worry about that now. Deacon shut the door and started his work. He had his small flashlight which he kept in his bedside stand. He knew exactly where to go and which wire to cut to silence the smoke alarms. The deed was done in seconds. It took only moments more to locate the water supply line to the sprinkler system, and to turn the valve completely off.

Now he had only to wait until after midnight, when the residents would be sleeping and the night staff would be busy, to sneak into the laundry room and start the blaze. But he didn't leave the room immediately. He liked the enclosed space, the wires, the pipes, all the equipment that was intended to make life in the facility safe and pleasant for its residents. Deacon grinned widely. Springwillow was no longer safe, and in a few hours the nursing home would be very unpleasant.

THIRTEEN

AT SUPPER, FONNIE had looked around desperately to find a table that didn't include any of the suspects. She lucked out when Alfreda called out to her, "Come sit with us, Fonnie. Cora's family took her out this evening so we have an empty place." She nodded her acceptance of the invitation and wheeled toward the group. Maude removed Cora's chair to make room for Fonnie's wheelchair.

Fonnie enjoyed the company and the meal. The salmon patties were lightly browned, the asparagus tender but not soggy, the creamed potatoes retained some lumps, and the rice pudding was topped with a dash of nutmeg.

The chitchat around the table covered such important subjects as which color was best for bluebird houses, the multiple uses of bottle caps, and if finger painting was more therapy than art. Fonnie relaxed. For a short while she was able to clear her head of murder and of evil and of her investigation.

After supper, Fonnie returned to her post by the aviary, and her mind returned to the matter at hand. Her thoughts stammered around in her head like the finches fluttered around their home, landing here and there and then taking off again. How can I learn more about each suspect? What were their lives like before coming to Springwillow? Who are they really? Then it came to her how she could find, if not all that information, at least some of it. All she had to do was read their social history. Fonnie remembered the social worker asking multiple questions and making detailed notes about her past: childhood, marriage, work, church. "We want to get to know you so we can serve you better," the social worker explained. This was the data she needed to know. But it was locked up in the admitting office.

The nurses would only have the medical history on their charts. The social history was kept separately. Fonnie even recalled which file the social worker had opened to place the life history of Fonnie Beachum in behind a giant *B*. If only there was a way to get to those files.

Sheba padded over to the aviary, studied the birds for a few moments, then jumped up to reclaim her favorite lap. Fonnie stroked the back of Sheba's head and the cat purred encouragingly. After a bit, Fonnie nodded. "Yes," she whispered to Sheba, "there is a way."

Fonnie knew the charge nurse in any facility always had access to master keys when the administrative offices were closed. And she remembered the first night she was here, she'd gone to the nurses' station and asked for an extra blanket. The nurse reached in a drawer, pulled out some keys. "I'll get you a new one from the storage room," the nurse had said.

"I need to get those keys," Fonnie told the sleepy cat. She lifted Sheba and placed her on the floor. "And you need to get gone. This is a job I have to do alone."

Fonnie wheeled slowly past the nurses' station. She could hear the nurse in the medication room, but there was no one at the desk. The door to the nurses' station could not be seen from the confines of the medication room. It was a half-door, only reaching as high as the counter. Fonnie wheeled up as close as she could get, checked for any observers, reached her hand over the door, opened the drawer. Her fingers grasped a ring of keys. She backed away quickly and tried to appear nonchalant as she headed for the back hall.

The hall was dark except for the light above the emergency exit. Fonnie was a little nervous. After all, she'd never committed an unlawful entry before. What if she was caught? She could lie and say that the door was unlocked and that she just wanted to check her file. Or better yet, she could feign a sudden attack of Alzheimer's and let the nurses deal with it. She tried to brush these thoughts away as she found the right key, opened the door, and wheeled in.

It was an outside room and there was still a smidgen of daylight filtering in through the lone window. But she knew the daylight would soon be gone, and she hesitated to turn on the overhead light. Instead she reached for the chain on a small desk lamp.

Fonnie moved over to the file cabinet. The files she wanted were in the top drawer of a two-drawer cabinet, within easy reach. She opened the drawer, skipped over the front of the alphabet, slowed down at the *F*s. Her fingers found Flynt—Calvin Flynt. She pulled out the file, swung it around to the circle of light on the desk, flipped to the social history section.

Fonnie was a speed reader. It was a skill she'd developed in nursing school to get her through the volumes of required reading. Now she skimmed the unimportant parts of the record, slowed down when she came to occupation. *Concordia Contractors. Home office—Raleigh. Retired after being injured in a construction accident.* Was that why he had to use a walker? Had the accident injured his mind, as well as his legs? He was certainly intelligent, but she'd known intelligent people who developed odd mental quirks, who became paranoid, who became dangerous. She knew it was possible.

She skimmed some more and halted at church preference. *Episcopal.* That information brought a smile to her lips. The Episcopalians she knew were not deep into Bible study. Then she frowned. But she seemed to remember they did have deacons in their church, and that they played an important role in the service.

Next of kin was listed as Ken Flynt in Dallas, his telephone number, postal and e-mail addresses were all listed. She slowly closed the file. Poor Calvin. Estranged from his only son.

Her heart told her to strike him off the list of suspects. Her brain wasn't so sure. What was that encounter in the computer room all about? Had she only imagined a threat of danger? After all, Calvin really didn't do or say anything to threaten her. Thoroughly confused by her conflicting thoughts, Fonnie returned Calvin's folder to filing cabinet.

Going down the alphabet she pulled out the one for Oliver Jefferson. His teaching career was outlined. A sister was listed as next of kin—so he had no wife or children. His church preference was Baptist. Oh, oh. Fonnie fidgeted in her chair. Some of her best friends were Baptists. Baptists had deacons in their churches, and they knew their Bibles, and many of them preferred the King James translation over more modern ones.

While she considered this latest revelation, Fonnie heard a scraping noise in the hallway. It sounded somewhat like a dull pencil sharpener or a piece of furniture being dragged across the floor. Fear shot through her body, squeezed her throat, knotted her guts—a different fear than she had in the computer room. There was someone in the hall, but she didn't know who or where or why. She was not within screaming distance of help, and there were no call bells in the staff offices.

Fonnie tried to still her breathing and her racing pulse. She slowly closed Oliver's file, slid it back into the cabinet, quietly closed the drawer. The sound had not repeated itself, but she knew she hadn't imagined it.

She waited. She watched the handsome wood-framed clock on the wall behind the desk. The big hand jerked one minute, two minutes. Whoever was out there, was not going to come in to challenge her. So it wasn't a staff member. And a visitor would hardly venture down a dark and empty hallway. That meant it was a resident, who, like herself, had no legitimate right to be there.

Fonnie waited another minute, heard nothing else except the ticking of the clock and the pounding against her chest wall. She had to get out of there. She'd have to forego seeing the other files. She scooted forward to turn off the desk lamp. The chain slipped out of her fingers and snapped back against the metal shade. The noise was just a dull ding, but Fonnie jumped as if she'd heard a gun shot. When her clobbered nerves crawled back inside her skin, Fonnie wheeled over to the door, cracked it open, and peeked out. The hall was empty. She scurried out and locked the door behind her. Now she had only to return the keys to their rightful place, and she could breathe again.

DEACON GAVE ONE last look around the maintenance room. Everything here was set. He opened the door, cringed as it again scraped across the floor, and slipped out. Then he saw the light in the admitting office. It hadn't been there when he'd passed by earlier. He figured the social worker must have come in to catch up on some work. He waited awhile and pondered what to do next. He figured that if he kept close to the wall opposite the office he could make his way down the hall without being seen. He ducked into the doorway of the craft room when the light in the office went out and the door opened. His eyes were adapted to the dimness of the hall, and he could immediately see who was coming out.

He watched with fury as Fonnie quickly wheeled away. What was that hussy up to? He bit his bottom lip as he watched her turn the corner. She was snooping. There was no doubt about that. What could she have learned in there? He shrugged. Oh, well. It didn't matter. Nothing would matter after tonight.

He hurried down the hall, peered around the corner. Fonnie was sitting by the nurses station. How could he get by her without being seen? Just then Gwendolyn and a babble of her visitors came out of the dining room with Styrofoam cups filled with coffee. He joined in behind them as they entered the day room.

FOURTEEN

THE NURSES' STATION was empty when Fonnie approached. She wheeled slowly up to the half-door, paused as if waiting for a nurse, scanned the area around. No one seemed to notice her as she returned the borrowed keys. She slid into a corner of the day room and waited until her galloping heart rate resumed a semblance of normalcy. She wanted to check her e-mail, but she didn't want any unwelcome company while she was there.

Fonnie searched the room for each of the suspects. Lucas was in his usual chair, legs jiggling and face half-hidden, this time by the covers of *Newsweek*. Calvin was waving a deck of cards and hailing Oliver over to the card table. Oliver nodded and headed in that direction. Jock appeared to be deep into a paperback novel. They all looked so innocent, she thought, but could one of them have been in hall D a few minutes earlier?

She turned her back on all of them and shuffled down to the computer room. There was nothing from Brian. Probably too soon to expect more information. Or Brian and his buddies may have been sidetracked from their investigation. She knew about spring breaks. They may have found a party—or started one of their own. With a few beers under their belts, they could easily forget about the mystery they were supposed to be solving.

But there was a short note from Amy that warmed Fonnie's heart.

Mom, Arrived home all right. Busy day tomorrow. Enjoyed our visit. Love you.

Amy wasn't one for sentimentality, but Fonnie could read over and under the words. She felt blessed to have a daughter and a grandson who truly cared about her.

Fonnie wrote Amy a brief message back. She assumed it would be read in the morning.

Dear Amy, Thanks for coming. Thanks for all you do. Have a good day. Love, Mom

Fonnie flipped off the overhead light, sat in the near darkness, replayed the day's happenings in her mind. The screens of the computers glowed in the room. Each screen flashed a different shade of green with a plethora of designs. Sometimes her brain felt like a computer screen saver: objects flying in all directions, no pattern, no sensible arrangement, and no end.

Her thoughts now were on her little venture into breaking and entering. That had been pure foolishness. What little she'd learned could have been gained simply by asking the right questions. From now on she'd confine her investigation to legal methods. Tomorrow she'd start again. She would find out all she needed to know.

Then another thought tumbled into her mind. Did she have enough time? Lit had died the same day his warning had been posted. The warning about the fire appeared this morning. Did that mean the villain intended to carry out his threat tonight? Maybe her time to unveil the monster was running out. And she was no closer to the truth than she'd been at the beginning. She still had the same four suspects. What could she do now?

The more she thought about the possibility of a fire, she realized how silly it was. Her eyes went upward to where sprinklers poked their heads out of the beige plaster ceiling. Above the door a smoke alarm hung, a silent sentry ready to sound its siren and flash its red light at the first sign of smoke. Surely if anyone thought he could burn down a nursing home, he must be mad.

Fonnie shuddered at her next thought. But that was the whole point. The man was mad. Mad as in vengeful. Mad as in crazy.

Fonnie wheeled herself slowly out of the computer room. She was exhausted: physically, emotionally, mentally. Her brain was beginning to spring leaks with her thoughts dribbling out like water through a colander. There wasn't anything else she could do tonight.

She paused in front of the nurses' station to catch her breath. The charge nurse was on the phone. "No. Ida Mae isn't working this evening. She went off duty at three o'clock." A pause. "I know that sometimes she works a double shift, but not tonight. She may have gone out with friends after work. Maybe you should check with some of them." The nurse had a puzzled look as she hung up. She turned to an aide passing by. "Ida Mae's mother says she didn't come home this afternoon. Did you see her when she left?"

The aide shook her head. "But we seldom see the day aides. They're doing their final rounds while we're clocking in and, when they're clocking out, we've started our own work."

Fonnie continued the trek to her room, but her mind was now on Ida Mae. So she still lives with her mother. That's nice. Girls so often nowadays can't wait to move out on their own. And of course, her mother is worried if she's late getting home. Young people have a hard time understanding a worrisome parent. But Fonnie remembered how it was. Amy sometimes got so caught up in her affairs she would forget to make a simple phone call to put her mother's mind at ease. That's probably what happened here.

It had been a long day, a tiring day. All Fonnie wanted now was to go to bed, cover up her head, and forget about everything.

IT HAD BEEN a long day, a tiring day. Deacon's mind was excited, while at the same time his body demanded rest. He decided he'd go to bed early, but he had no intention of sleeping. As soon as he could, he'd get up and carry out his plan.

A BLAST OF THUNDER roused him, followed by another and another. The very room seemed to reverberate with the sound. The thunder was interspersed with the racket of rain dousing the windows. It took a moment for Deacon to orient himself. He glanced at the digital clock at his bedside. It was nearly two. He had slept. He had overslept. There was no further time to waste. He quietly slipped out of bed, inched his way to the partially opened door and peered out. Red call lights were on above doors on both sides of the hall. Aides were scurrying to answer them. The thunder must have awakened several other residents. Now what? He couldn't leave his room with the hall crawling with people. Maybe the storm would lessen soon and things would return to normal.

He remained at the door, watching the aides hurry up and down the hallway. He heard one aide call out to the charge nurse, "Gwendolyn wants to know if she can come to the day room and watch TV. She can't get back to sleep."

"Sure. Why not? I doubt if anyone is going to sleep much more tonight."

"And Tillie's crying. She says her baby doll is scared and wants a glass of milk."

"So give her some milk. Do anything you can to calm these people down."

In a few moments Deacon saw Gwendolyn shuffling down the hallway. She was wearing a housecoat as big as a tent, covered with red geraniums that looked like they should be adorning a grave site. He could picture the blobs of flesh bobbing around under the garment.

He looked away in disgust. That's what Ida Mae would have been like in twenty years, he thought. He actually had done her a favor and saved her from that ignominy.

As the rain continued, Deacon sighed. He might as well go back to bed. He'd have to put his plan on hold for now. Another crash of thunder made him flinch. He looked out the window at the torrent of rain, shook his head in disappointment. Then his spirit lifted. He would write another warning to remind them of what was coming. He knew just what his final message from God would be: RESERVED UNTO FIRE AGAINST THE DAY OF JUDGMENT.

That day had only been postponed, not canceled.

FIFTEEN

MONDAY DAWNED CLEAR. The rains had skedaddled during the early morning hours leaving flooded sidewalks, drooping leaves, and oodles of puddles. Fonnie was awake during the worst of the thunder, but had still managed to get a fair night's sleep. She awoke refreshed, her body and mind ready for the day. She was up and out of the room before Lila stirred. She watched the day shift come in, and the night shift depart.

There were few residents in the day room. Probably most would be sleeping later than usual due to the interrupted night. Fonnie hoped to talk to Jean this morning to elicit more information about Lit. Specifically, Fonnie wanted to find out if Lit had shown any symptoms of infection in the days prior to his death, and if he ever had previous episodes of severe hyperglycemia. But when the director of nursing came in, she was immediately intercepted by Gloria.

"We're short staffed today. Ida Mae hasn't shown."

"She didn't call?" Jean asked.

"No. And that really burns me. These young kids have no sense of responsibility."

"Have you called her home yet? She may have overslept."

"I was just going to. And I may give her a piece of my mind."

Jean unlocked her office door, unloaded a briefcase of papers onto her desk, and then went back to the nurses's station. Gloria finished the call and turned to Jean. "That was her mother. Ida Mae never came home last night, never came home after leaving here."

"Strange."

"Her mother wants me to check her time card and let her know what time Ida Mae clocked out."

"I'll do it and call her back. You check the time sheet and try to get someone else to come in. We can't work shorthanded."

Fonnie figured that it would be a while before Jean would be free to talk. And since it was still several minutes before time for breakfast, Fonnie decided she would visit the birds. She hadn't wheeled far, though, before Jean came back with a time card in her hand. She waited until Gloria got off the phone again. "This is strange. Ida Mae didn't clock out yesterday at all."

"Like I said, these young people can't take responsibility. She probably had a hot date after work and forgot all about the time clock. You ought to dock her an hour—just to teach her a lesson." Gloria started toward the medication room. "Oh, I called Beth to come in. So we'll be all right."

"Fine. Well, I'll call Ida Mae's mother. I can't imagine what got into the girl. She always seemed reliable to me."

IT SEEMED TO FONNIE that the birds were perkier than usual, their songs merrier, their soaring gayer. Or maybe it's just that everything seems brighter and happier after a bad storm. She stayed by the aviary until she heard the tiny gong of the breakfast bell. Then she wheeled down the hall, greeting sleepy-eyed residents on the way.

She pulled up to an empty table and hoped no one would join her. Instead, Jock came in, jerked a chair out, plopped himself down. "Good morning, Sunshine," Fonnie said. "Get up on the wrong side of the bed?"

"No. It just takes a while for my natural good cheer to kick in."

"Then the storm didn't keep you awake?"

"Slept like an innocent baby. Nothing like a good strong sleeping pill."

"Aren't you afraid you'll become addicted to those pills?"

Jock gave her a wry smile. "What difference does it make? It's not like I'm going anywhere."

Fonnie shrugged. She'd lectured people for years on the danger of addiction, but she wasn't going to pursue the subject. She was more interested now in asking some particular questions, and she was through trying to be causal about it. "Jock, what church do you go to?"

"Hoot, gal. You're not fixing to convert me, are you? 'Cause if you are, I won't take kindly to it."

Fonnie laughed. "I don't attempt the impossible. I just need the information for a little project I'm working on." It sounded rather lame, but it was the best excuse she could think of on the spur of the moment.

"If you must know, I belong to the universal church of nature. We have no creed, no services, and no collection plate."

"But you know the Bible so well."

"I also know the teachings of Buddha and the Koran. I agree with all of them."

If he's telling the truth, Fonnie thought, *then he certainly wouldn't be posting warnings about vengeance and fire. If he's telling the truth.*

It was after breakfast when Fonnie saw the latest warning. She'd gone by the bulletin board earlier without even looking at it. Now as the message stared out at her, she felt that Satan himself was taunting her. RESERVED UNTO FIRE AGAINST THE DAY OF JUDGMENT. She reached up with her right hand, snatched the evil paper from the board, folded it quickly in half, and slid it under her buttocks. Surely some of the staff must have seen the messages. Did they just consider them silly and harmless? That was another thing she would ask Jean about.

One thing she was sure of now, though, was that Jock was not the author of these missiles of hate. He may be cantankerous and bitchy and outspoken, but he wasn't sneaky. If he had something to say, he'd say it. He wouldn't hide behind a shield of religiosity.

Suddenly Fonnie felt better. She'd narrowed her field of suspects down to three. She was finally making some progress.

IT WAS NEARLY TIME for her PT session. Fonnie wheeled as quickly as she could to her room. She hid the obnoxious message next to the previous one. She had every intention of turning them over to the police at some point.

ANDY WAS WAITING for her. Today his scrub suit was a regal purple, the color Fonnie imagined would suit King Solomon. But she knew that Solomon in all his glory could not have been as handsome or as charming as the man in front of her. "Fo-on-nie. You're looking lovely today. Ready to try walking the bars?" Fonnie's head jiggled up and down like an eager puppy. She was ready to try anything with him.

"This is my assistant, Elga. She's going to help us today." A skinny blonde with big eyes and thick lips reached out and shook Fonnie's hand.

Elga guided the wheelchair to one end of the parallel bars, Andy buckled a heavy belt around Fonnie's waist and grasped the back of the belt. Fonnie clenched the bar with her right hand while Andy curled the fingers of her left hand around the bar.

He then helped her to stand.

"Ready?"

Fonnie inhaled deeply, smiled widely. "As ready as I'll ever be."

Andy stood along the outside of the bars, supported her body with the belt when she moved her right foot, after which he would shove her left leg forward with his knee. It was exhausting. It was humiliating. It was the hardest work she'd done in her life. This set of bars was only six feet long. It seemed like six miles. All the time Elga followed right behind her with the wheelchair waiting to catch her bottom if she toppled backward. She hated the chair. She hated the bars. And for a moment she hated Andy and Elga for making her try to walk.

At the end of the bars, Andy skillfully lowered her into the chair. Fonnie shut her eyes tightly, forced back the tears. She didn't trust herself to speak. Andy seemed to understand.

"It'll get easier."

Fonnie managed a half smile. "It'd better."

DEACON STUDIED THEM from a shadowed doorway across from the physical therapy room. Earlier he'd watched Fonnie as she read his latest warning. Her fear was unmistakable. Good. That's what he wanted. He wanted her to be afraid: afraid of the future, afraid of what would happen next. He wanted them all to be afraid, but no one else was taking him seriously. They would. They all would.

He'd seen Fonnie tear the message down, hide it in her chair. What was she up to? First her questions, then her snooping in the admitting office, then snatching the warning. *I can't let her start blabbing,* he thought. *I've got to get her alone.* A half-paralyzed old woman wouldn't be hard to silence.

He smirked. Yes, he repeated to himself, a half-paralyzed old woman wouldn't be hard to kill.

SIXTEEN

BIG AND HIS COUSIN came in the front door just as Fonnie wheeled back to the day room. Big was carrying a lovely flower arrangement of white lilies. Gloria came out of the nurses' station and greeted Big with a hug. "We missed you."

Big grinned and shoved the flowers toward her. "Lit's flowers. Put in chapel."

The cousin explained. "That's the arrangement your administrator sent to the funeral. Big thought it would be nice to bring them back here so everyone could enjoy them. He wants to place them in the chapel if that's all right with you."

"Of course. I'll go with you and we'll find just the right spot to put them."

A few moments later, Fonnie saw the three of them rushing back. They looked like they were about to upchuck: their eyes half-shut, their hands over their mouths, their legs trembling. Fonnie had seen reactions like that before. Sometimes coming off a roller coaster, sometimes coming out of a bar, almost always coming out of a morgue.

Big and his cousin slumped in the nearest chairs.

Gloria ran to Jean. Jean ran to the phone. By the time Fonnie shuffled over close enough to hear, Jean was ending the conversation. All Fonnie heard was, "Please don't use your siren. It'll upset the residents too much."

That's all it took to jump-start Fonnie's curiosity. It was like a race horse straining at the bit. What was going on? Sirens meant either police or ambulance. She quickly eliminated fire trucks since there was no move to evacuate the facility.

Fonnie did her best to waylay Jean for information, but the nurse ignored her as she rushed over to where Big and his cousin sat. After a few minutes of earnest conversation, Jean motioned Keisha to take Big to his room, and the cousin started for the front door.

Fonnie forgot all about being tired following her therapy session. Instead she seemed to have energy to spare as she galloped her wheelchair at top speed to cut off Cousin before he got past the rubber plant.

"Pardon me," she blurted out. The man turned and looked at her in surprise. "I couldn't help noticing that Big was upset. Was Lit's funeral too much for him? We're all so very fond of Big. I do hope he's going to be all right."

"Yes. Yes, I'm sure he'll be fine. It's just that he's had a shock." The man shook his head and rubbed the back of his neck. "We both had a shock."

"Oh? What happened?"

Fonnie held her breath waiting for the man to answer.

He finally did. "A body," he whispered. "A body in the chapel." He stepped away from her. "I've got to go. I've got to get out of here."

A spasm of fear rippled through Fonnie's brain. Whose body was in the chapel? Her eyes skidded around the day room. Were any of its regular occupants missing? Gwendolyn was in her usual chair in front of the TV, King Tut in her lap; Lucas was in his corner; Lila and Calvin were absorbed in the megapuzzle; Jock looked like he was dozing; Tillie was cuddling her baby doll. And Fonnie had seen Oliver a few minutes earlier in the dining room arranging the chairs in proper order. She assumed the other active ladies were busy in the craft room. So who was the body?

A black and white police car drove up. Two uniformed policemen bolted in as Cousin scurried out. Jean's concern about a siren upsetting the residents was rather irrelevant. What did she think the appearance of police officers would do? Necks craned, scared whispers sprinted around the room and down the halls, feet hurried toward the chapel until politely but firmly turned around. Questions, fear-filled rumors, and speculations engulfed those in the day room.

More police cars arrived with more uniformed officers, and with some men and women in plainclothes. All the staff seemed to have disappeared. Perhaps they were being questioned by the police, Fonnie thought. It was nearly an hour later when Jean's soft voice came over the intercom. "There will be a resident meeting in the dining room in ten minutes. All residents who are able to attend are asked to do so."

JEAN STARTED BY TELLING the gathered group that a terrible accident had occurred. "Ida Mae Feeney has been found dead. At this point we don't know what happened. It seems that she probably died yesterday afternoon." Jean's voice faltered, her eyes blinked. The room was still. A dozen sets of rheumy eyes strained through bifocals. Hearing aides were turned up. Shadowed minds tried to make sense of what the nurse was saying. Jean went on. "The police are here because they must investigate any unexpected death. If anyone has information that may be relevant, you are asked to come to me or to the administrator and we'll see that you have a chance to talk to the police." Jean finished in a flurry. "Now it's almost lunchtime so those of you who usually eat in the dining room may stay. The rest of you are asked to return to your rooms." Then almost as an afterthought, she added, "The chapel will be closed off. Please do not attempt to go through the yellow tape."

Members of the group started to stir, some raised their hands, a couple blurted out questions. Jean shook her head. "No questions. That's all I can tell you now." She turned and the back of her uniform disappeared down the hall.

Fonnie stared at the table top, toyed with a napkin. Her thoughts seemed to layer themselves. She was actually surprised that she was able to think logically at all. She repeated Jean's short speech in her head and came to several conclusions. Something terrible had indeed happened, but it wasn't an accident. Ida Mae had been murdered. And the police knew that. The yellow tape Jean referred to was crime-scene tape. In her heart Fonnie knew the same person responsible for the other deaths had also killed the aide. Even though there were no similarities, she knew this to be true. The first two deaths had been made to look as if they were natural. Apparently, Ida Mae's had not. Hannah and Lit were residents, Ida Mae was an employee. But the same murderous mind had planned and carried out all the executions. Now at last Fonnie would have a chance to tell her story and her convictions to someone who would listen.

For the first time since Jean left the room, Fonnie lifted her eyes. Some of the residents sat alone, staring into space, perhaps afraid or embarrassed to share their thoughts. Others huddled together, murmurs and whispers floating above their tables. Calvin and Gwendolyn and Oliver was one such cluster. Their heads nearly met in the center of the table. Fonnie couldn't hear what they were saying, but one after another, their lips moved, their heads bobbed in agreement.

Fonnie's attention centered on Calvin. She had almost deleted his name from the suspect list earlier, now she was nearly sure he couldn't be the murderer. Maybe a man dependent on a walker could have smothered fragile Hannah, but surely he couldn't have struggled and subdued and killed a young, strong girl like Ida Mae. She caught herself midthought. If there *had* been a struggle. Maybe the killer hadn't given the girl a chance to struggle. Fonnie was determined to find out all the details. She would share her information with the police, but in return she would ferret out the details from them.

Lucas was sitting in his usual place next to Tillie and her baby doll. Tillie seemed particularly agitated. Fonnie wondered how much she understood of what Jean had said. Lucas got up, went over to the side bar where coffee, iced tea, and water were available to anybody at any time. He brought back two glasses of tea and held one glass to Tillie's lips, urging her to drink. She gave him a grateful smile. Tillie was lucky to have a friend like Lucas. Most people, like Fonnie herself, just ignored her.

Fonnie glanced up as Jock scraped a chair across the floor, pulled it up next to her, and flopped down. Fonnie was glad to see him. She needed someone she could talk to, someone she could trust. "Well, gal. What do you make of the news?"

She shuddered. "It's horrible. Poor, sweet Ida Mae. She was always so cheerful, so bouncy."

"Except for the last couple of days."

"You noticed it, too? I remarked about it to Keisha. Ida Mae seemed distracted, jittery. Keisha thought it might be due to the diet she was on, not eating right. Come to think of it, she may have been taking diet pills. They tend to make some people jittery."

"Or she may have had a fight with her boyfriend. She

mentioned her boyfriend to me once when I asked if she was married. She said, 'No, but I'm thinking about it.' She went on to say that he was a pretty demanding guy and she wasn't sure she wanted to spend the rest of her life taking orders from him."

"But her boyfriend wouldn't have come here. Not while she was working."

"He may have. Visitors come and go Sunday afternoon. No one would have noticed. Maybe she saw him come in and hauled him into the chapel so they could talk without being interrupted. Maybe they argued, he lost his temper, strangled her."

"Strangled? Is that what happened?"

"That's what I heard. You know, for an old gaffer, I have excellent hearing. I heard one of the policemen say 'garroted' which means strangled. Actually it means, strangled *with* something. Like a rope. Not just bare hands."

Fonnie felt her stomach lurch. *So I was right,* she thought. It was planned. People don't just happen to have a garrote handy when they take a notion to kill someone. Should she tell Jock what she suspected? Was she ready to make him her confidante?

The arrival of Salisbury steak, mashed potatoes, and black-eyed peas made it possible to delay that decision. Fonnie was pleased that this was the kind of meal she could manage with one hand. She always hated to ask for help to cut a pork chop or a slice of roast beef. But today she needed no help. The Salisbury steak easily crumpled with a touch of her fork, the potatoes and peas slid onto her spoon with no problem. She did face a bit of a dilemma trying to spread margarine on her Parker House roll. The piece of bread seemed to take delight in avoiding her aim, skidding around as if it had sprouted skates. She finally succeeded by taking her right hand and lifting her left hand onto the table top. She leaned forward to anchor her left arm, placed the roll in her listless hand, and triumphantly slathered it with the golden spread. She knew Jock furtively watched her efforts and was glad he hadn't intervened. Her self-esteem needed every little victory she could muster.

Jock reached for the ketchup bottle and buried his peas under a red river. Fonnie shook her head slightly. "You can't even taste the peas with all that goo."

"That's the idea. I never have figured out why Southerners are supposed to like black-eyed peas. The rest of the country has more sense than to eat them."

"Are you sure you're not a Yankee in disguise?"

"Afraid not. I happen to love grits and hush puppies and fried catfish." Jock shoveled a scoopful of peas and ketchup into his mouth and quickly followed it with a gulp of iced tea. He wiped a dribble of ketchup from his chin and stared at Fonnie. "You know, you've been asking a lot of questions lately."

"I have?"

Jock nodded. "And now it's my turn. Where did you grow up? Did you have a good marriage? What church do you belong to? If we're going to be good friends, I need to know more about you."

"Fair enough." Fonnie twirled some gravy around in

her potatoes before she looked up. "I could use a good friend just about now." She studied the man across the table from her. His soft brown eyes gazed back at her through thick lenses, his bald head gleamed in the light of the overhead fluorescent bulbs. In spite of his blustery temper, Fonnie sensed that here was a good man, a man she could trust.

"Not much to tell. I grew up down east, went to nursing school in Charlotte, came here to work. Married a local boy." Fonnie paused in her recollections, then went on. "Yes, I had a good marriage. He was a good person, a good provider, a good lover—even a good cook. And I still miss him." Fonnie slid back in her wheelchair and a smile played around her lips as she concocted the next bit of history. "Now about the church I belong to. It's called the Church of the Universal Compassionate Supreme Being."

Jock slapped his napkin over his mouth. Fonnie could tell he was trying not to laugh. He didn't quite succeed. A slight snort escaped that he attempted to camouflage by dropping his knife. By the time Jock recovered his knife from the floor he'd also recovered his dignity. "I reckon this is the same supreme being that sees no evil, hears no evil."

Fonnie became serious. "Oh, He sees evil. He sees a lot of evil. And He expects us, His children, to stop those who do evil."

"That's a tall order."

"Yes, I only hope I'm up to it."

Fonnie caught sight of Jean in the hallway talking to a plainclothesman. She assumed he was the detective in charge. She quickly excused herself from the table, wheeled toward the door, called out to the nurse. Jean was obviously annoyed at the interruption. "What is it?"

"I need to talk to the detective. I have some information."

The man looked down at her from a height of at least six feet, dark eyes alert, notebook in hand. "And that would be?"

"Could we go somewhere and talk privately?"

The man nodded. "Jean has offered her office for me to use. But I need to finish talking to the employees. I'll let you know when I can get to you."

DEACON WAS A LITTLE UPSET about Ida Mae's body being found so soon. It might put a crimp in his plans. Nothing seemed to be going right with him lately. The thunder and the ensuing commotion last night had kept him from carrying out his scheme. Now there were cops crawling all over the place. Surely they'd be gone by tonight and he could get on with his work.

But he overheard what Fonnie said to the detective. What information could she possibly have? Would he have to deal with her first?

SEVENTEEN

FONNIE WASN'T HAPPY about the wait, but knew she had no choice. The detective would get to her after he talked to all the employees who worked with Ida Mae. She assumed other detectives or police personnel were questioning the aide's family and friends. Fonnie was still undecided how much of her suspicions to reveal to Jock, so instead of going back to him, she scuttled to the computer room. She planned to e-mail the latest development to Brian. That should get his cop juices flowing again.

To her surprise there was mail waiting for her.

Dear Gram,
Sun peeking out now so will be heading for beach soon. Just wanted to update you. Ben's dad says Jowoski doesn't have a first name, just went by initials J.C. Also he found out that Jowoski spent time in alcohol rehab and after that never returned to work.

Frank found Oliver Jefferson in state retirement file. Nothing particularly interesting there. Spotless record. The file mentioned his charitable work which included building Habitat for Humanity houses.

*Calvin Flynt was awarded a big settlement for
injury suffered on the job, his legs were messed up
by a runaway machine. Before his accident, Flynt
was an amateur magician, gave benefit shows for
worthy causes.*

Nothing yet on Lucas Parker.

*Frankly, Gram, I don't see anything here that
suggests a motive for murder. Maybe we'd better
forget the whole thing. I'm going out now to catch
some rays.*

Love, Brian

Fonnie deleted the message when she finished
reading. She didn't print it out as she didn't want to take
a chance of anyone else reading it. She changed her
mind about telling Brian of the latest murder. He probably wouldn't be in until late to pick up her message
anyway. Maybe she'd wait until after talking to the detective. There might be more to tell then. She thought
for a moment about e-mailing Amy with the news, but
rejected the idea. No use worrying her.

So now there was nothing for Fonnie to do but sit and
ponder and speculate. She wheeled out to the day room,
found a spot behind a Ficus plant and speculated. Poor
Jock. She wasn't really surprised to find out he'd been
an alcoholic. She'd known several alcoholics: fine, wonderful people, educated, talented. She understood how
it could happen. She switched her train of thought to the
other information about Jock. He didn't have a first

name, eh? She vowed right then that she would find out what the initials J.C. stood for.

And what about Lucas? Was no news good news as far as he was concerned? Perhaps. Perhaps not.

Not much new on Oliver. Spotless record. Charitable work. Nothing wrong there.

That left the new knowledge about Calvin. A big settlement would account for his having money. He seemed to get around very well with his walker, but if his legs had been badly injured then he probably would not be able to stand or balance himself without it. And what was the other thing Brian had mentioned? Fonnie reread the message in her mind. Flynt was an amateur magician. Magician to Fonnie meant sleight of hand. Could they be evil hands? Did Hannah remember some magician tricks that turned out to be evil? Fonnie shook her head at the ridiculous thought. Calvin had performed at charity benefits. Nothing evil about that.

IT WAS LATE AFTERNOON when Fonnie was summoned to Jean's office. The detective was leaning back in the swivel chair, his tie loosened, his shirt rumpled, his eyes weary. He sat up, managed a smile, and held out his hand. "Lieutenant Evan McElroy."

"Fonnie Beachum."

Tiny lines encircled his dry lips as he pushed out a mouthful of air. It sounded like a tired, collapsing balloon. "Now what was it you wanted to tell me?"

He glanced at his watch and Fonnie could imagine

how a contestant on a game show might feel who had exactly three minutes to name all the presidents. She had so much to tell him: about Hannah and Deacon and Lit and the Bible messages and about Ida Mae being skittish and about the men who might be suspects. Where should she begin?

He waited, eyes half-shut, making half circles with the swivel chair. After a few moments he looked up. "So?"

So Fonnie started her tale. She started at the beginning and got as far as Lit stealing candy when Lieutenant McElroy interrupted her. "Mrs. Beachum, I thought you said you had some information regarding the murder of Ida Mae Feeney."

"I do. But it all ties in together. I'm trying to tell you that we had two murders here before Ida Mae. And the same person is responsible for all of them. And that person is a resident here and I have his fingerprints and…"

"Excuse me, Mrs. Beachum, I appreciate you wanting to help, but I really don't have time to listen to anything irrelevant to the case." The detective rose, towered above her, started to turn her wheelchair around.

"Lieutenant McElroy. This is relevant. I insist you listen to me. I know I'm an old woman. Half my body is paralyzed. But I am not demented. Now you just take that little notebook of yours and make some notes. I'll try to be succinct."

The detective roared in laughter. "My, aren't you the feisty one." He sat back down, opened his notebook. "All right. I'm listening."

Fonnie started again. This time she gave him just the facts. The fact of Hannah's pillow being on her bedside stand, the fact that Lit's blood sugar wasn't high enough to result in death, the fact that Ida Mae appeared nervous, the fact of the biblical quotations on the bulletin board.

Lieutenant McElroy listened politely, made notations. When Fonnie paused for a long breath, he said, "Thank you for your input. I assure you I will look into what you've told me."

But Fonnie wasn't through. "The warnings. I think we have to take the warnings seriously. This madman is planning on burning down the nursing home."

"I understand your concern, but even if someone was to start a fire in this building, it wouldn't get very far. Everywhere you look, there are smoke detectors. I have a cigar in my pocket that I'd give a week's pay to be able to light up right now, but if I did that detector above the door would go crazy. And if that wasn't enough, as soon as the rooms got hot enough, the sprinklers would cut loose. No one can burn this place down. You don't need to lose any sleep over that. As far as the rest of your story, I'll check it out." He stood up and this time he whirled Fonnie's wheelchair out the office door before she could object.

"But I haven't told you the names of the suspects."

"I'll get back to you tomorrow on that."

"Promise?"

"Promise. I have to go now."

Fonnie scowled. "But you're leaving someone here? Someone to stand guard?"

"There's nothing to guard." The detective rubbed the back of his neck and forced a smile. "We've gotten what we need from the crime scene, although we'll leave the tape up. Thanks for your input. I'll be back after I've had a chance to go over everything."

After Lieutenant McElroy left, Fonnie sat in the hallway deep in thought. There was so much she hadn't told him. But he'd promised to get back to her to-morrow. Maybe then she would have a chance to ask him some questions also. What was used to strangle poor Ida Mae? Did she put up a struggle? Was she molested? If she knew more about the crime, she could better determine which of her suspects was the most likely perpetrator.

The tinkling of the supper bell broke her chain of thought. It was just as well. She needed some respite. Her brain was beginning to feel like fried mush.

Fonnie inched her way down the hall toward the dining room. She found an empty table in a corner and hoped no one would join her. The last thing she wanted to do was to attempt a cheery conversation. Apparently she wasn't the only one who felt that way. Most of the regulars sat gloomy faced and sad eyed. The usual lively buzz was reduced to a low drone. The silent kitchen crew served them methodically, without their usual sunny comments.

Perhaps it was the lack of noise that made Fonnie pay

more attention to her other senses, especially the scents emanating from the kitchen. Tonight's menu was soup and sandwiches. Fonnie inhaled deeply of the thick garden odor of split pea soup, the tantalizing aroma of bacon floating in the green lake, the pungent cheddar lathered with deli mustard between slices of whole grain bread. And something else. What was the other smell that teased her nostrils? Fonnie turned her head toward the kitchen to get a better whiff. It reminded her of backyard barbecues, of summer evenings, of roasted hotdogs.

Smoke. There was definitely a smell of smoke coming from the kitchen. Nothing threatening, not overpowering, but it was certainly smoke. She motioned to one of the kitchen helpers. When the woman got close enough, Fonnie whispered, "I thought I smelled smoke. Is there something wrong in the kitchen?"

"Not anymore." The woman shook her head grimly. "But you won't be having any peach cobbler tonight. Maggie burned it. She made all kinds of excuses. Said she's been so upset about the killing of that young girl and about the police being around here all day asking questions. She forgot to set the timer and it burned to a crisp. So dessert tonight will be store-bought chocolate chip cookies. But you would have died laughing at us trying to get all that smoke out. We opened the back door and all of us were waving towels like mad. Then I got a fan that's kept in the craft room. That helped a lot." The woman turned to go, then looked back at Fonnie. "I'm surprised you noticed it. I don't think anyone else has."

"I have a very sensitive nose. I can smell better than a coon dog hot on the trail of his master's supper."

"Yeah, sure. Well, I'll bring your cookies out in a little bit."

When she finished eating, Fonnie wheeled out to the day room and over to the megapuzzle. Anything to get her mind off the real-life puzzle. Mt. Kilimanjaro must have been completed because a new one was on the table just beginning to take shape. Fonnie studied the cover of the box. It showed a small cabin in the woods, leaves in their festive fall colors, a bonneted woman hoeing in the garden, and a thin tendril of smoke coming from a chimney. A peaceful early Americana scene. Fonnie found some dove gray pieces and erected the stone chimney. She nodded in satisfaction—a good few minutes work.

She leaned back and noted the genesis of smoke at the top of the chimney. That might be a good place to work. Before her fingers found the next piece of smoke, however, her brain took a U-turn back to the dining room. Smoke. There had been smoke in the kitchen. But no smoke alarm had sounded. Why not? She remembered Lieutenant McElroy said that even a lit cigar would set off the alarm. Surely a burnt peach cobbler should have done so.

Wheeling around, Fonnie made like a racecar back down the hall. The dining room was empty, the kitchen crew was doing their last cleanup chores. She scooted over to the door. The same woman who had talked to her earlier came out. "Want some more cookies? They were pretty good even if they were bought ones."

"No. I just want to ask a question. Did the smoke alarms go off in here earlier? When you said you were waving towels?"

"No-o. Come to think of it, they didn't. There wasn't nary a sound of any alarm." The woman turned. "Maggie, come here a minute." Maggie moseyed over. "Maggie, how come the smoke alarms didn't start screaming when you were doing your fire dance?"

Maggie scowled. "Don't know. But they didn't. I hadn't given it a thought, but now that you mention it, they sure didn't go off. Reckon somethin's wrong with 'em?"

"I don't know," Fonnie said. "But I intend to find out."

Fonnie's next stop was the nurses' station. Jean had finally left to go home. The charge nurse that night was a part-timer. Her name was Dana and she'd only worked one evening since Fonnie had been at Springwillow.

Dana was busy charting medications when Fonnie came up to the counter. The nurse glanced over. "What can I do for you?"

"There seems to be a problem with the smoke detectors in the building."

"What makes you say that?"

Fonnie explained the kitchen situation. Dana didn't seem concerned. "As long as there wasn't any damage done, why worry about it?"

Fonnie tried to control her irritation with Dana's inane reply. "Because maybe *none* of the alarms are in working order. And if there was a fire, we could all die before we realized what was happening. Don't you think that's enough to worry about?"

Dana gave Fonnie a sweet smile, a smile Fonnie knew was as fake as the nurse's long crimson fingernails. "And what am I supposed to do about it?"

"Call the maintenance man over here to check them out."

"I don't want to call him out at night. I'll leave a note for him to check them in the morning."

"That might be too late."

"Don't be ridiculous. Nothing's going to happen tonight. Besides, it's probably just the one in the kitchen that's not working. I'm sure the others are fine."

"But what if they're not?" It wasn't often that Fonnie met a nurse she didn't like. She'd worked with all kinds during her career, and could get along with almost anybody. But she was getting pretty aggravated with this young gal.

Fonnie well remembered working nights at the hospital, and that she never hesitated to call maintenance for any kind of problem that arose. Dana was either stubborn or stupid. Maybe both. Fonnie tried another tack. "I guess if you knew how to do it, you could check some of the detectors out yourself."

"Well, I *don't* know how. They're hooked up somehow to the electrical system. Or do you think I ought to start a fire in a trash can to test them out?"

"Of course not."

"Good. Now, if you'll excuse me, I've got to get back to my work."

Fonnie felt hot tears well up behind her glasses. No one believed her. Everyone looked at her as if she was daft. And why should anyone believe her? She was just a silly old woman, seeing bogeymen behind every door. Maybe the stroke *had* affected her mind. At any rate, there was nothing else she could do. She'd tried and she'd failed. She wheeled away from the nurses' station. She might as well go to her room and go to bed.

But Hannah's voice stopped her. *His God was always mad.* And whoever Deacon was, his God was still mad: mad enough to kill three people, mad enough to disable smoke detectors and then start a fire. A madman with a mad God who had to be stopped.

With a burst of adrenaline born out of determination, Fonnie hustled over to the bulletin board. This time she snatched an official notice from the board that highlighted an eight hundred telephone number.

Back at the nurses' station she tapped loudly on the counter. Dana looked up. "Now what?"

"Please set the phone over here so I can make a call."

Dana picked up the phone and placed it on the counter within Fonnie's reach. "Local number?"

"No. As a matter of fact, it's a Raleigh number. I'm calling the Elder-Abuse and Neglect Hotline."

Dana dropped her pen, shoved the chart she was working on out of the way, and yanked the phone back.

Her hands trembled. "What are you talking about? There's been no abuse or neglect here."

"I think nonfunctioning smoke detectors qualify as neglect. And I'm reporting it as such."

Fonnie could sense the turmoil going through Dana's mind. The young nurse was probably weighing Fonnie's right to make a phone call against the repercussions of such a call. She shoved the phone back. "Go ahead. It's after hours. You'll just get an answering machine, and will have to leave a message."

"Right. But when the message is heard in the morning, this place will be crawling with inspectors and ombudsmen. And your sweet buns will be in the hot seat. Even if all the other smoke detectors are found to be in working order, the administrator will be very unhappy with you. It's not good policy for a nursing home to draw attention to itself. Once those inspectors get down here, they could look in every medical record, behind every door, in every personnel file. Who knows what they might find?"

"All right." Dana's voice was thick with outrage. "You win. I'll call Jimmy over to check things out. I hope you're satisfied."

Fonnie didn't answer. She pivoted her chair around and took refuge behind the rubber tree plant. Appalled by her own audacity, it was several minutes before she could breathe normally again. She looked around the day room and wondered if any of the other occupants had heard her exchange with Dana. If so, it wasn't evident. Most of them were watching the evening news on TV. Had Ida Mae's death been reported to the media? Perhaps not yet. The police might be keeping quiet about it as long as possible.

Fonnie wanted to position herself so she would see Jimmy when he came in the employees' entrance. But she also wanted to stay out of Dana's way. The charge nurse was feeling none too friendly toward her at the moment. She chose a spot opposite the nurses' station, but with a clear view of the long hall. She picked up a magazine and pretended interest in it. Jimmy ambled in as if he was taking a stroll in the park, chatted with Dana, then meandered down the hall and around the corner to the maintenance room.

A few minutes later, he tore back down the hall at twice the speed he'd gone before. He zoomed to the nurses' station, leaned over the counter, gave Dana a frantic wave.

Fonnie swivelled her chair in that direction and wheeled as fast as she could. She nearly ran into Jimmy's legs. He ignored her. Dana tried to shoo her away. But Fonnie wasn't about to be shooed anywhere. She leaned forward as Jimmy gave his report in a hoarse whisper. "The wire's been cut."

"Cut? You mean a wire broke loose? That's the problem?"

Jimmy shook his head like an angry bull. "I mean, cut. Deliberately. And that's not all. The valve to the sprinklers was turned off." Jimmy's breaths came in short gasps. "I didn't touch anything after I noticed the valve. The police might be able to get fingerprints."

Dana reached out and clutched Jimmy's arm. "Police? Fingerprints? I don't understand."

"I don't, either. But something bad is going on here."

Fonnie refrained from saying anything. It gave her no pleasure to be proved right. Her only satisfaction was in knowing a disaster had been avoided. But she still didn't know the identity of the madman. Then the question popped into her brain, did Deacon know *her* identity? Did he know who had foiled his plans?

DEACON HEARD ENOUGH to know that his carefully laid plans for revenge had been thwarted. He glared at Fonnie with hatred. She would pay for this. Yes, she would pay.

EIGHTEEN

THE POLICE CAME. Crime scene investigators came. The administrator came. Even some firemen came. Fonnie heard them all praising Dana for her alertness. She basked in the attention, saying that the safety of the residents was her first concern. No one asked Fonnie any questions. That was all right. Fonnie would tell her story to Lieutenant McElroy in the morning, ask him to compare the fingerprints on the biblical messages she'd confiscated with those found in the maintenance room. Fonnie just wanted Deacon caught; she didn't care who got the praise for doing so.

The administrator's soft, comforting voice came over the intercom, reassuring the residents that everything was under control. He suggested they retire to their rooms and try not to worry. He explained that there was a slight problem with the smoke detectors, but that it was being corrected. He also said that a policeman would stay on duty at the nursing home throughout the night so they could rest easy.

Fonnie yearned for her bed, for some rest. But there was one more thing she needed to do before calling it a day. She wanted to e-mail the latest developments to

Brian. He was probably partying, and she didn't know when he'd get her message, but she wanted to know if he'd found out anything else about her suspects. The thought of going to the computer room by herself, however, was a little scary.

Most of the residents were following the administrator's suggestion and were straggling to their rooms. Fonnie noticed that Jimmy, an electrician, and some firemen were still in the hallways testing the newly repaired smoke alarm system. That boosted her courage. She needn't fear with all those people around.

Her message to Brian was short. She told him of Ida Mae's murder, but didn't mention anything about the disabled smoke detectors and sprinklers. Then ended with, *Do you have anything to add about the suspects? Let me know as soon as possible. Wish you were here. Love, Gram.*

THE PRESENCE OF a police officer in the building quieted Fonnie's fears. She was drained of all energy, of all thought, and slept like the proverbial log. If she dreamt at all, she didn't remember it when she awoke Tuesday morning. In fact, she had a hard time remembering anything when she first awoke. She had the feeling that something had happened yesterday, something dreadful, but she tried to push it away.

Her brain, however, wouldn't allow her much respite. Soon yesterday's events engulfed her mind, her emotions: Ida Mae strangled, fire alarms sabotaged, Deacon still out there. Fonnie pushed her call bell. She had to get up. She had to talk to the detective. She wished so badly that Brian were here. She wished her safe, peaceful world would return so that all she had to worry about was learning to walk, not chasing a murderer.

WHEN FONNIE GOT to the day room, she noticed two police officers conferring behind the aviary. The man was crumpled and haggard, the woman was crisp and alert. Apparently one was going off duty and the other coming on. She guessed the police planned to keep officers stationed here as long as necessary to ensure the safety of the residents. Through the front windows she could see a patrol car slowly driving by. *That's good,* she thought. They must be patrolling the entire area. It gave her a secure feeling. Deacon would not have a chance to run away unseen. And as soon as she had a chance to talk to the detective, she was sure her suspects would be fingerprinted, the evil one revealed.

Fonnie waited until the off-duty officer left, then wheeled over to talk to the remaining one. The officer looked awfully young to Fonnie, but then nearly everybody except her fellow residents looked young these days. "Pardon me, miss," she started, caught herself and started over, "Pardon me, officer. Could you tell me if Lieutenant McElroy will be coming in this morning? I really need to talk to him."

The officer shook her head, reddish curls flopped back and forth, gentle green eyes smiled at Fonnie.

"Sorry. I have no idea. I'm Julie Daniels. Can I help you with anything?"

Fonnie longed to say, "Yes." She imagined this girl would actually listen to her, take her seriously, believe her. Instead she replied, "No. But please remind him that he promised to get back to me today about some information I have. The name is Fonnie Beachum. Will you tell him that?"

"Of course. I'll call the office and relay the message."

That made Fonnie feel better. Now to get a good breakfast and face the day. But before going to the dining room, she headed for the computer room. She told herself there was no reason to be afraid. There were plenty of people around, and Officer Daniels was nearby.

Had Brian gotten her message last night? Would he respond? He had and he did. Fonnie read the words with a sense of thankfulness. *Dear Gram, I'm on my way. Be careful. You may be in danger. I love you, Brian.* She dismissed the warning about danger, but she was thrilled with the first and last sentences. The e-mail had been sent at 7:15 a.m. That means he should be here by lunchtime, maybe sooner, Fonnie thought, as fast as he drives. Marvelous. It would be so good to have someone by her side she could really confide in.

Breakfast was a quiet affair. Apparently several people decided to eat in their rooms. Of her suspects, only Calvin was in the dining room, and he chose a seat in the corner with his back to the rest of the room. Clearly he didn't want to talk to anyone.

Fonnie contemplated her French toast without enthusiasm. The edges were burnt while a dollop of uncooked egg stared at her from the center. She doused it liberally with cinnamon, and emptied the entire pitcher of syrup on it. She closed her eyes and dug in. After the first bite, she opened her eyes and smiled. It wasn't half bad. Two cups of coffee later, she thought she was ready for whatever the day would bring.

When Fonnie wheeled back out to the day room, Keisha reminded her what was next on the agenda. "Andy ordered whirlpool exercises for you on Tuesdays and Thursdays. You go on down to your room and I'll be down shortly to help you change into your swimming togs."

"They're not swimming togs. Just an old pair of shorts and a T-shirt. And I'm not sure I want to start the whirlpool today. The police detective is coming back to talk to me again."

"There'll be plenty of time for you to talk to the police. From the looks of things they'll be around for a while. And it's important for you to get as much exercise as possible. Now no more excuses. Scoot."

Fonnie scooted. Back in her room, she dug in the drawer and got out the shorts and shirt Amy had brought. Fonnie hadn't worn shorts in probably twenty years. She didn't intend to walk around with the back of her legs looking like the Mississippi River and its tributaries. But for some reason she had kept a few pairs hidden away in an old chest, perhaps to remind herself that she once had pretty legs, and hadn't minded flaunting them.

Unlike many people whose waists expanded to match their years, Fonnie weighed the same as she had as a young bride. Admittedly, the weight had shifted southward a few inches, but she was sure the shorts would still fit.

While Keisha helped her dress, Fonnie quizzed the aide about what scuttlebutt was making the rounds regarding Ida Mae and what happened to her. Keisha denied knowing anything, hearing anything, even thinking anything. "Surely, you have some opinion. You worked closely with her. Did she say what was bothering her? Was she afraid of somebody?"

Keisha pulled the T-shirt roughly over Fonnie's head. "Like I told the police yesterday, I don't know a thing." She draped Fonnie's bathrobe over the back of the chair, tossed a bath blanket over her knees, spun the wheelchair around. "Let's go dump you in the water."

Keisha skidded the wheelchair down the hall, through the day room, past the nurses's station, and around the corner toward the therapy room. Fonnie saw Sheba leap off the couch and trot after them. "For heaven's sake, Keisha, we're not running a race. Stop and give Sheba a ride. She wants to go with us."

"Cats don't like water," Keisha grumbled, but she slowed down enough so Sheba could jump on Fonnie's lap. "She'll hightail it back down the hall when she hears the whirlpool. It makes more racket than a washing machine."

They passed the craft room where Ginger and a group of ladies were talking and giggling and cutting out quilt squares. They continued on down hall D. Fonnie heard the whirlpool before they even entered the PT room.

"You already have it filled and running?"

Keisha nodded. "Yes, ma'am, the tub is full of nice warm water, ready to massage every muscle you have."

Contrary to the aide's prediction, Sheba didn't run off. Instead, the cat jumped on the brick rim of the tub and watched the churning, gurgling water in apparent fascination. Keisha parked the wheelchair parallel to the edge of the tub, put the brakes on, and helped Fonnie to her feet. Fonnie sat on the rim, and Keisha deftly lifted Fonnie's legs over into the water. A shiver of delight went through Fonnie's body. "Oh, that feels good."

"Now keep your right hand on the edge and slowly lower your body," Keisha instructed, raising her voice to be heard over the splashing water. "I'm right here if you need help."

Fonnie didn't need help. She slid slowly, sensually, hedonistically into the bubbling cauldron. She leaned her head back and grinned at Keisha. "This must be sinful. It feels so absolutely wonderful."

Keisha laughed. "You must have heard the same preacher I did one day. He said that if anything feels good, then it's wrong. Of course, I didn't believe it for a minute. But in case it is true, I'll leave you now to enjoy your sin."

"Fine. Come back in about thirty minutes."

"Will do. If you need me before then, just push the call bell. It's right over there to your left, below where Sheba is sitting. I guess she's going to stay and keep you company." Keisha shoved the wheelchair back out of the way.

"Leave the door open when you leave." Fonnie said. "I don't like being shut up in a room."

"You can't even see the door from where you are. You wouldn't know if it was shut or not."

"I'd know. Now quit pestering me and let me float away in sinful pleasure."

Fonnie sat on the projection built into the tub for a bench. The surface was rough, purposely so, she assumed, to prevent people from slipping off. It also, however, made it more difficult to move around the tub. Using her right foot to propel her, and using her right hand to lift her bottom up, she was able to maneuver around to the back side of the tub until she sat opposite Sheba. She wanted to keep an eye on the cat in case the feline decided to do something uncatlike, such as jumping into the water. But the tumbling froth seemed to have a hypnotizing effect on the cat. Sheba sat perfectly still, wide-opened eyes glued to the scene below her.

Fonnie squirmed down lower in the water until the bubbles reached her chin. A faint whiff of chlorine teased her nose. Her T-shirt and shorts ballooned out in front as jets on either side of her pulsated the water. Her left arm, which usually dangled lifelessly by her side, started to rise slowly to the surface. Fonnie was enchanted as she watched the force of the water elevate her shriveled limb. She glanced down at her left leg and it, too, was moving slightly.

Fonnie recalled a Bible verse from her Sunday School days. *And the Spirit of God moved upon the face of the waters.* That's exactly how she felt. The love of God was bubbling up all around her. She leaned her head back, shut her eyes, was one with the sound and the feel of the water.

As she rested there, Fonnie realized there were actually two sounds to the whirlpool; one was the drone of the motor, and the other was the noise the jets made as they propelled the water around. The din at first was rather overpowering, but gradually it became almost as soothing as a lullaby. Her body, her mind, was as relaxed as a baby in a rocking cradle.

After a few moments, however, Fonnie jerked herself alert. She had something to do besides floating like the Queen Mary at dock. Both her body and her brain had work to do. Andy had instructed her in some range of motion exercises to strengthen her left side, and while she was doing the exercises she wanted to go over in her mind what she knew about Deacon and compare it to each of her suspects.

Her need to identify Deacon throbbed in her brain, not only to name the guilty person, but to clear the innocent ones. She realized she might be going through unnecessary angst. Maybe all it would take to solve the case was to match fingerprints—from the chapel and maintenance room to either Oliver, Lucas, or Calvin. But her mind kept gnawing at the clues like a tenacious dog worrying a bone. Maybe there was something she'd missed.

So while she worked her muscles: contracting, extending, pushing, circling, Fonnie's mind was doing cartwheels of its own. Whoever had disabled the smoke detectors and sprinkler system had to know how such things worked. Surely it wasn't common knowledge passed along in the male genes like understanding football plays and actually enjoying baiting a hook. But, she recalled, Harrison had this huge fix-it-yourself book that he used to pore over, so maybe the knowledge was there for the taking.

Fonnie stopped in mid-wrist rotation, as the compass needle of her mind swung straight at Calvin Flynt. Calvin worked in construction. He would know about sprinklers and alarms and how to cripple them. He'd won a big settlement after being injured in a work-related accident. Was the accident on the up-and-up? Had he been involved in some kind of fraud? If so, that would have been fairly recently. Was there also some dark secret way back in his youth that Hannah knew about?

Then there was Lucas Parker. Why had he lied about his occupation? At least *she* was sure he'd lied. She couldn't imagine anybody buying insurance from him. Wasn't it strange that Brian's buddy hadn't been able to find out anything at all about Lucas? Surely a computer genius, who could hack into the governor's breakfast menu, could come up with some info: a service record, a credit record, something. And there was that incident with the bird. Was it a demonstration of violence or merely a reflex action?

What about Oliver Jefferson? He and Hannah were from the same area of the state. Had she known something dark about him before he became the kindly school teacher? Maybe he had an obsession for something besides neatness, something that had landed him in trouble. Brian mentioned that Oliver worked on Habitat for Humanity houses. Could he have learned about fire detectors and sprinklers?

She didn't intend to include Jock Jowoski in her ruminations. She thought she had ruled him out earlier. But one thing nagged at her. Why hadn't he returned to his practice after rehab? Was there something in addition to alcoholism in his background?

Fonnie shook her head. It was about time to call it quits. Her muscles and her head both ached. She looked at the clock. Keisha wasn't due back for another ten minutes. Fonnie decided instead of ringing the call bell, she would just relax the rest of the time.

She emptied her brain of all activity except for listening to the harmony of the effervescing water. Then in the midst of the watery concert there came the question again. Why had Ida Mae been so jittery? She almost acted like she was afraid of someone.

Again Fonnie's mind forced her to go back over each of the suspects in connection with the aide. She recalled when Ida Mae had referred to Calvin as "spooky" and "creepy" and that she didn't like the way he looked at her. It was no secret Calvin was an admirer of the ladies—both old and young. Fonnie had thought it was more smoke than fire. But had he actually made improper advances to her? And had she threatened to blow the whistle on him? If so, what connection would that have to do with the earlier deaths? Maybe there wasn't a connection. Were there two murderers at Springwillow?

Fonnie waved her hands in the air in exasperation. In so doing, she splattered some water on Sheba's head. The cat, who was still sitting on the edge of the tub, came out of her trance, shook her head wildly, and glared at Fonnie.

Fonnie laughed. "Sorry about that. I know cats don't like water, but I don't like being stumped, either. There has to be an answer to all this mess. I can't give up now."

Sheba either nodded her head in agreement or decided she couldn't be bothered and bobbed her head again in meditation. Fonnie went back to her puzzle.

Oliver's face floated across the churning water. He'd remarked to her that Ida Mae thought he was crazy and would get all jumpy if he was in the room when she was making his bed. Was there more to it than that? Did Ida Mae have a deeper reason to fear him?

What about Lucas? And what about Jock? Fonnie tried desperately to remember anything further Ida Mae had said about any of the suspects.

A faint memory stirred in the back of Fonnie's brain, jiggled around some, then plopped into place. She sat straight up. That must be it!

She knew now. Fonnie knew who had frightened

Ida Mae, knew who had killed her, knew who had the evil hands.

She had to get out—get to the police—tell them what she knew. Fonnie started scooting back around the tub, toward the call bell. She had gotten only a short distance when she heard a discordant sound. A swish, a rustle. It took Fonnie a moment to identify it as the door closing. Had someone in the hallway absentmindedly pulled the door shut? Or perhaps Keisha hadn't opened it wide enough and it closed by itself. Fonnie strained her ears, listened carefully for steps. She didn't hear any, but she sensed someone was in the room with her. Someone had come in and shut the door.

Should she call out? Maybe someone had wandered in inadvertently. It might even be a police officer. They were in the building checking things out. Maybe he or she, thinking the room to be empty, would turn around and leave.

Fonnie was still debating with herself when a faint shadow slithered in front of the tub. A second later, a form pushed the shadow forward. Fonnie stared at the man in front of her. She needed no introduction. She sat face-to-face with Deacon.

NINETEEN

FONNIE FOUGHT TO control her breath and her expression, but there was nothing she could do about her pounding pulse. She opened her mouth and was surprised how calm her voice sounded, even at the higher volume needed to be heard.

"Hello, Lucas. What are you doing here?"

Lucas's face twisted into a sneer. "You know damn well, bitch." Gone was the shy, meek man with the jiggling legs, hiding in the corner. Here was the evil man that Hannah had recognized, his eyes dark with hatred, his powerful hands clenching and unclenching at his sides. "You'll pay for what you did." His voice became louder, deeper, more menacing. "Vengeance is mine."

Fonnie forced her eyes away from the enraged face, lowered them to where Sheba sat and to where the call bell beckoned to her. The bell was only inches away from Lucas. It was an ocean away from her. Lucas probably wasn't aware of the bell, or at least of its location. She had to reach it before Lucas carried out his vengeance. It was her only hope.

She could scream, but would anyone hear? Not likely over the noise of the whirlpool and with the door shut.

The only other people on the hall were in the craft room, laughing as they went about the handicrafts. They probably wouldn't pay any attention if they did hear anything. It was doubtful any of the police officers in the building would be close enough to hear her cries for help. She had to stay calm, keep Lucas talking, figure out a way to reach the call bell.

Fonnie refocused on the madman in front of the tub. She scrunched as far back as possible on her seat. "What do you mean, I'll pay for what I did? What did I do?"

"You spoiled everything. God wanted me to use these hands to bring the judgment fire. And I would have done it. It would have been a beautiful fire. The flames leaping up, nothing to stop them. The smoke curling around each bed, choking, strangling my enemies." Lucas lifted his eyes to the ceiling, as if even now he expected flames and smoke to be climbing up the walls, engulfing the room, meting out vengeance.

"What enemies? You have no enemies here. The people here are your friends." Fonnie had no illusions that her remarks would make any difference to Lucas, but she felt she had to keep talking, and to keep him talking.

Lucas's tight lips spread into a thin smile. "Jesus understood about enemies. He said, 'He that is not with me is against me.' People have been against me all my life. Laughing at me, insulting me, refusing to listen to my warnings. But God told me a long time ago that I would have vengeance."

Fonnie doubted if now would be a good time to

remind Lucas that Jesus also said we were to love our enemies. Somehow she knew the madman called Deacon would have his own take on that command.

Lucas's tight smile was suddenly replaced by a scowl of disappointment. "God promised me revenge. And I would have had it. It was all planned. No alarms to give warning, no water to dowse the fire."

"You had a good plan, all right." Fonnie felt her throat closing in, but she took a deep breath and went on. She didn't know if she could stall him long enough, but she had to try. "A clever plan. How did you learn about smoke alarms and sprinklers?"

"You can thank the state of North Carolina for that. They have all kinds of work programs in prison. It's called 'rehabilitation' and the big guys get all excited when a prisoner learns a useful trade. Ain't that a hoot?" Lucas stepped closer to the tub, and Fonnie saw his Adam's apple do a little wobble. "Yeah, I had a clever plan. But you spoiled it. You got in my way."

"Like Hannah and Lit. Did they also get in your way?" Fonnie knew Lucas intended to kill her just as he had killed the others. She intended to stop him, but if she wasn't able to, then at least she'd go into eternity knowing why all this had happened.

"I came here to kill one person. Took me years to track him down. And just when I decided I had enough barbital to put him to sleep forever, that blasted woman recognized me. I couldn't take a chance of her actually remembering."

While Lucas talked, Fonnie reached down with her right hand, pushed up on the seat to raise her buttocks and slid over to the right a few inches. Lucas didn't seem to notice. It hardly seemed likely to Fonnie that she could slide all the way around the tub to the call bell without being noticed, but she had to try.

"So you smothered her with her own pillow?" Fonnie determined to keep up her interrogation even though she was close to tears. It was almost more than she could bear, thinking about being in the very next bed to Hannah while this monster suffocated her old friend.

Lucas gave a smug nod. "I had to."

"Why? What did Hannah know?"

"Never mind that. You're the one who knows too much now."

Lucas sat down on the rim of the tub. Fonnie felt sure he was gauging the distance between them. It was farther than even his long arms could reach. She knew, however, he could very easily step into the whirlpool, overpower her, hold her under the water. She was determined not to show the fear that threatened to overwhelm her. "You know you can't get away with killing me. It's one thing to smother a helpless old woman in the middle of the night. It's quite another to drown someone in the middle of the day."

"Oh, I'll get away with it. I'll just say I was passing by the door and heard you call for help. I ran in and tried to save you from drowning. I even got in the tub and attempted to lift you out. But, poor thing, you must have suffered another stroke, and my efforts were in vain." Lucas nodded his head in satisfaction, and slid along the tub's edge a little. "I may even get a hero's medal for trying to rescue you."

When Lucas moved, Sheba came out of her trance. Instead of staring at the water, she now scrutinized the man who had intruded on her meditation. The cat didn't look happy about it. Fonnie wanted to shoo Sheba away out of possible jeopardy, but didn't know how to do it without alerting Lucas to the cat's presence.

Fonnie kept up a pretense of composure. If she could keep his attention long enough, Keisha would eventually come back. But would that put Keisha in danger? He'd killed one young, strong girl. What would stop him from attempting it again?

She had to keep talking. "But why Lit? He didn't know anything about you."

"That simpleton. He rummaged around in my drawer, looking for candy. Well, he found candy all right, but he found my plans, too. He might have blabbed about the pictures of fire. So to keep him quiet, I gave him more candy."

"Laced with poison?"

"You can call it poison if you like. I called it a giant sleeping pill."

"The barbital?"

"The fool was so greedy I'm sure he didn't notice the added ingredient in his chocolate bar. And the nurses never questioned what had knocked him out. They just assumed it was his diabetic problem. People see what they want to see, don't they?"

Yes, Fonnie thought sadly, *and all this madman sees are enemies.* She had managed to scoot another six inches closer to the side of the tub where the call bell was located. The trouble with that maneuver was it also brought her closer to Lucas. Her only recourse was to keep asking questions. So far he seemed more than willing to answer them.

"And Ida Mae? What did she do to you?"

"That little hussy? She knew something. I don't know what, but every time she saw me, she acted like I had leprosy. She wouldn't even make up my bed if I was in the room. No one is going to treat me that way."

Fonnie knew her supposition about Ida Mae had been correct. "The only thing Ida Mae knew was that you were the cruel person who had killed a lovely little bird. She couldn't get that terrible picture out of her mind. She told me she would never forget what you'd done."

"Well, she got what she deserved." Lucas put his fingers in the water, played with the bubbles, splashed some her way. "Now it's your turn."

Fonnie cringed, stifled a cry.

Lucas must have read the fear in her eyes and it pleased him. He grinned. "I knew you were up to something when you started nosing around—asking me where I grew up, what kind of job I had."

"Which you lied about. You could have come up with something more believable than an insurance salesman."

Lucas ignored Fonnie's sarcasm. "You know, at first I thought you just wanted to be friends—good friends. I've known a lot of women who couldn't keep their hands off of me. I figured you were lonely, needed a boyfriend. I could have gone along with that. I was never one to shy away from a little hanky-panky. There's always a way to find a place and time." He let some water dribble through his fingers as he watched her reaction.

Fonnie's stomach lurched at the thought. Lucas had just brought the definition of "dirty old man" down to sewer level.

"Is that how Tillie repaid you for your kindness?"

Lucas slapped the water with his right hand. Sheba stood up and arched her back as water trickled off her whiskers. "How dare you say that! Tillie was like a sister to me. I would never have touched her."

Fonnie gaped at the man in amazement. *It seems,* she thought, *that even Satan has a line he won't cross.* "But you were willing to let her perish in the fire along with the rest of us. Or didn't you think of that?"

"It couldn't be helped. It's called collateral damage. But enough about Tillie. You're the one we're talking about now." Lucas stood up, clenched both hands into tight fists. "You thought you were too good for me. I saw you cozying up to those other fellows. And then I knew what kind of woman you really were. You were just like my mama. She'd puff up her hair, fix up her face, anything to get a man's hands into her pants. Well, my daddy took care of her and I decided I was going to take care of you.

"But then I thought, why not take God's vengeance on all of you? All of you had laughed at me, were too good for me, didn't treat me right. And I would have. Except for your meddling."

Fonnie knew her time was running out. She had to reach the call bell. She thought maybe she could stand on her right foot, throw herself forward and push the bell before Lucas reacted. She knew he would try to drown her, but it was her only chance.

Before Fonnie could execute her plan, Lucas's long arms reached across the whirlpool, went under the water, grabbed her left leg—the leg she could not kick. He pulled steadily. She felt her bottom sliding off the seat, felt the water rising over her chin. Fonnie kicked wildly with her right foot, tried to grab hold of the back of the tub with her right hand. The evil hands grasped her ankle like a vise, pulling her forward, dragging her down.

It was too late to scream, even if anyone could have heard her. She raised her right leg and pounded her foot against his arms. His grip tightened. Fonnie's head plunged under the churning water. She gave a giant heave with her shoulders, propped her right arm on the bottom of the tub and managed to get her nose above the water. She gagged and spit and prayed.

At that moment Sheba jumped into the fray.

TWENTY

SHEBA TOOK ONE LEAP, landed on Lucas's head, dug into his scalp. Lucas howled. His hands dumped Fonnie's leg and flew upward, splashing some water over the side of the tub. He whacked and swatted at the cat. Sheba dug in deeper. He poked, swiped, flailed. He cussed and damned and called on hellfire. None of it deterred Sheba. She answered back in a caterwaul that would do credit to a banshee. But she didn't relax her hold. She had her quarry and she wasn't going to let loose.

Fonnie gawked in fascination and awe. She was too absorbed in the drama to realize she now had her chance to reach the call bell.

Lucas stood upright and shook his head wildly. His hands tore at the yellow beast who had him in its grip. His feet stomped in front of the tub, making little puddles on the floor. Sheba let out another yowl. Lucas's feet slipped out from under him. He plunged forward.

Fonnie watched in horror as Lucas splashed into the water and as his head struck the brick edging on the side of the tub. Sheba released her hold and Lucas's head sank slowly beneath the bubbles.

Another feline howl brought Fonnie's eyes back to

the cat. Sheba vaulted from Lucas to the rim of the tub without getting a drop of water on herself. Then she sat quietly on her haunches as if expecting a pat on the head for her good performance.

An unusual gurgling noise brought Fonnie's attention back to Lucas. He lay face downward in the water.

Instinctively Fonnie tried to reach him. She had to pull his head up, save him from drowning. It wasn't a conscious thought. It was simply what she needed to do.

Summers in her youth she'd worked as a lifeguard. Then she'd become a nurse. Saving lives was what she did. And she had to save Lucas.

She scooted as fast as she could around the side of the whirlpool, pushing with her right hand and foot and dragging the rest of her body. She reached down, got hold of the back of his shirt, tugged and pulled. She positioned her body so she could pull him back against her and then she placed her hand under his chin. She lifted his face above the bubbles.

Fonnie didn't know how long he'd been under water. She had lost all track of time. But his face wasn't blue. She slid her fingers over to the side of his neck. She thought she felt a faint carotid pulse. Then she saw his chest rise slightly. He was alive. Now she had to ring the call bell and get some help in here before he regained consciousness.

But she couldn't reach the bell. She was imprisoned behind Lucas. His back laid against her chest. She had to find a way to move over to the bell without letting go of his head. She tried lifting her buttocks, tried pushing with her right foot. She couldn't budge. Her arm was trembling with fatigue.

Where was Keisha? Why didn't somebody come? Brian might be driving up soon. Would anyone tell him she was in the whirlpool?

Fonnie tried not to think about who it was she held up on her arm, about all the evil he had done. It wasn't up to her to judge. God and the courts would do that. She had only to turn him over to the authorities. It had always been her job to save life. But, she reflected, it hadn't always been possible. There were times when she'd been told to "let go." Maybe this was one of those times. Fonnie knew she was still in danger. Lucas might have been only stunned by the blow to his head. He could wake up any moment. And if he did, he would finish his murderous intention.

So why couldn't she let him go? She had only to remove her arm from under his chin. He would sink under the water, and she'd be safe. The world would be safe from this evil madman. No one would know that she could have saved him, or would blame her for not trying.

No one except Fonnie Beachum. Fonnie, the nurse, who had taken an oath to devote her life to those committed to her care. Right now, Lucas, aka Deacon, was in her care, and she had to do everything in her power to save him.

Fonnie gasped for breath, tightened her grip, and prayed she'd be able to hold on until help arrived. Her arm trembled, her whole body ached, her sense of claustrophobia was beginning to smother her. The sounds of the motor and water jets seemed to get louder, like a train roaring down the track in her direction. She shook her head to clear her mind, took several quick breaths, and glanced over to Sheba. The cat was still on alert.

"Sheba," Fonnie whispered, "when we get out of this mess, you and I are going to take a good long nap."

Instead of an answering purr, Sheba emitted a plaintive mew. At the same time Fonnie felt a movement across her chest. Was Lucas coming around? Or was the water just moving his body? She twisted her head to see more of his face. His eyes were closed, his mouth sagged, his breaths were shallow but even. As she studied his face, and wondered how life had brought him to this point, she saw his left cheek twitch. His eyelids began to flutter, his left hand moved a little.

"Oh, my God!" Fonnie gasped. "What do I do now?"

But the decision was taken out of her hands. Sheba vaulted across the tub in one long leap. The cat's intended destination was probably Lucas's head again. But she fell short. Sheba crashed down on Fonnie's right arm, plummeting both herself and the arm under the water.

Sheba desperately tried to cling to Fonnie's arm, to gain a foothold somewhere, to escape the turbulent pool. At the same time, Fonnie gaped at Lucas's head as it slowly slid back under the water. His arms floated upward, almost as if they were waving goodbye.

Fonnie entered a dreamlike trance. A trance in which

her body refused to move. Her right arm hung motionless at her side, as useless as her left one. She could do nothing to save Lucas this time.

Nor could she help Sheba.

With one last caterwaul of protest, the cat abandoned her attempt to crawl up Fonnie's body to safety. Sheba tumbled into the gurgling foam. The pulsating jet sprays swirled the tiny body around, and Fonnie saw her friend disappear beneath the bubbles.

Water trickled down Fonnie's cheeks. She didn't know if the drops were from the sloshing whirlpool or from her tear ducts. She closed her eyes, tried to block out everything. It didn't work. The evil man and the heroic cat both did a death dance in her brain.

Fonnie struggled to come out of her dream state, but her mind resisted. It took another sound—a different sound than the water jets—to bring her back to the real world. It was the sound of splashing. Fonnie sat bolt upright, brought her right arm up to ward off an attack, and scanned the tub for movement. She could make out the faint outline of a body close to her feet. It wasn't moving.

The sound came again and Fonnie smiled in relief when she located its source. A head of matted yellowish fur was following two diminutive paws paddling for dear life. Sheba reached the side of the tub where the faucet was located. With the skill of a gymnast, the cat reached up, grabbed the faucet with one paw, hauled her back legs up, leaped over the rim. The jump landed her in the seat of Fonnie's wheelchair where she promptly hid under the bath blanket. Fonnie breathed a prayer of thanks for Sheba's survival.

Now it was time to let go of the nightmare. She knew that by now Lucas had completed his trip from this world to the next. His tortured soul was either at rest or at the gates of Hell. In either case, it was out of her hands.

She slid around the tub and rang the call bell.

TWENTY-ONE

FONNIE HAD BEEN WRONG. A scream *could* be heard above the noise of the whirlpool. At least Keisha's scream was. It was a perfect scream: high-pitched, piercing, unending. It zoomed out the open door, down hall D, invaded the cozy craft room, sent shock waves through the quilters. Ginger sprinted toward the screech, and upon reaching the scene, added her alto voice to the soprano. They both were pointing to the body curled up at Fonnie's feet.

Fonnie hushed them with her, "Damn it, girls, shut up and get me out of here!" They hauled Fonnie to the edge of the tub, and Keisha pushed the wheelchair around. "Be careful of Sheba," Fonnie warned. "She saved my life."

Officer Julie Daniels rushed into the room followed by several ladies from the craft room. "What's going on in here?" the policewoman demanded. Keisha shook her head as she wrapped Fonnie in her bathrobe. Ginger pointed to the pool. Officer Daniels radioed for help and at the same time shooed the onlookers away.

Fonnie sat shivering in her wheelchair. She was swathed in her bathrobe and covered with a fuzzy bath blanket, but still she was cold. Keisha had gathered Sheba up when Fonnie sat down and now she placed the cat in Fonnie's lap. "You two look as if you need each other," the aide said.

Ginger pushed Fonnie to the other side of the PT room, behind the walking bars. Someone turned off the whirlpool and the voices of the police officers and the nurses drifted her way.

She waited there while several police officers dragged Lucas out of the tub, placed him on a sheet, and covered him with another one. Fonnie had given them a brief, very brief, explanation of what had occurred. Now she waited for their further questions. Jean intervened for her with the police. "Can't we take Fonnie back to her room and get her into some dry clothes? You can talk to her there." The police agreed.

KEISHA HELPED HER into jogging pants and sweatshirt and suggested she rest in bed for a while. It sounded like a good idea to Fonnie. She lay back, tried to empty her mind of everything connected with Springwillow. Back to a time when spring meant she could read the words of Solomon and revel in them. Some of the words floated tenderly through her head. "Winter is past. Flowers appear on the earth. The time of the singing of birds is come." Perhaps some day she'd be able to erase this ghastly spring from her mind. Or perhaps not.

Brian burst into the room, covered the distance from

the door to her bed in three long strides, flung his arms around her.

"My God, Gram, what happened? The nurse said you almost drowned." He pulled back a little, studied her carefully. "Are you all right?"

To Fonnie's surprise she exploded in a torrent of tears.

"No," she sobbed. "I'm not all right. Things may never be all right again."

Brian grabbed a handful of tissues from his grandmother's bedside stand and started blotting her tears.

"It's okay, Gram. I'm here now. You can tell me all about it."

Fonnie sniffed, blew her nose, attempted a smile, patted his hand. Before she could get started on her gruesome account, Officer Daniels entered the room. She approached the bed slowly and quietly, worry evident on her face. "Do you feel up to making a statement now?"

Fonnie pulled her pillow up behind her back, sat up straight, and nodded. "Yes. I can talk now. Can my grandson stay? He needs to hear it, too."

The officer smiled at Brian and introduced herself. "I'm glad you're here. Mrs. Beachum needs someone with her. And you may stay while she's making her statement if that's what she wants."

Brian sat down on the edge of the bed and took Fonnie's hand. The policewoman pulled up a straight-back chair and took out her notebook. Fonnie began by explaining to her about the two suspicious deaths prior to Ida Mae's murder.

"I told all this to Lieutenant McElroy yesterday, but I don't think he gave my account much credence." Officer Daniels made no comment. Brian stirred to a more comfortable position. "Lucas Parker was one of my suspects from the beginning, but there were others also."

Brian's body twitched. "Lucas was the one? No one mentioned Lucas to me when I came in."

"Yes. But I can only tell the story once, so be quiet and listen."

Brian grinned. "Yes, ma'am. Go on."

Fonnie went on. She told about going to the whirlpool to do her exercises. She told of Lucas coming in and accusing her of spoiling his plans. She tried her best to repeat what he had said word for word: that he had come to Springwillow to kill one person, his confession of killing three others, his disabling the smoke alarms and sprinkler system, his plan to burn down the nursing home, and his intention of killing her.

Officer Daniels interrupted from time to time to clarify a point. "He didn't say who it was he came here to kill?"

"No. He kept rattling on about those who messed up his plans and how he had to get rid of them."

When Fonnie came to the part about Lucas grabbing her leg and trying to pull her under the water, Brian squeezed her hand and the policewoman seemed to be holding her breath. Fonnie gave a low laugh remembering Sheba's charge on Lucas.

"How can you laugh at a time like this?" Brian said.

Fonnie explained in detail about the tiny cat battling

the fearsome giant and soon both her listeners were nearing smiles.

But Fonnie sobered when she told of Lucas hitting his head, being unconscious, and slipping under the water, of how she tried to save him.

"Save him?" Brian exploded. "Why in hell would you want to save him? He tried to kill you."

Fonnie shook her head. "I don't know. I just had to try. But in the end I couldn't." She told how Sheba had jumped on her arm, forcing her to drop Lucas's head.

"That cat deserves a medal," Brian said. "Where is she now?"

Fonnie smiled. "Probably curled up someplace quiet to catch a catnap. Which is exactly what I need."

"We'll leave you alone shortly," Officer Daniels assured her. "Anything else we should know right now?"

"One more thing." Fonnie turned on her side and retrieved two sheets of paper from her bedside drawer, and handed them to the officer. "I'm sure Lucas's fingerprints will be on these warning messages." She lay back and sighed. "That's the end of my story. Now what do you know? Have the police found out anything about Lucas yet, his background, what turned him into a monster?"

"It's a little early for that," Officer Daniels answered. "The medical examiner is still with him. When he finishes he should be able to corroborate your version of events."

Brian stood up, faced the policewoman, his face red with fury. "What do you mean her 'version of events?'

And why should she need corroboration? She told you what happened. That crazy guy tried to kill her, just like he killed the others."

"I know. I know. I only meant that we have to wait for the official report about the cause of death. Of course, Mr. Parker's fingerprints will be matched against those found in the chapel and in the maintenance room." Her soft voice calmed Brian and reassured Fonnie. "And his prints will be fed into our database. We'll know a whole lot about Lucas Parker before the day is over.

"Thanks for your cooperation, Mrs. Beachum. Oh, and Lieutenant McElroy left a message for you. He said he'd be by this afternoon to see you. Until then, you try to get some rest."

Officer Daniels had barely left when Keisha came in, bringing Fonnie's lunch tray. "I didn't think you'd feel up to going to the dining room."

"You're right. Thank you. I don't feel up to eating much, either, but I'll give it a try."

Keisha arranged the tray on the over-bed table, and removed the plate cover revealing a steaming portion of chicken casserole topped with a cornmeal crust. A tossed salad and a piece of hot apple pie completed the meal. Fonnie sniffed appreciatively. "Maybe I am hungry after all."

Keisha spoke to Brian. "Sir, I'd be glad to bring you a tray also if you'd like one."

Brian shook his head. "No thanks. I had a late break-fast." He helped Fonnie with her napkin, made sure she could reach everything, shuffled restlessly. "If it's all right with you, Gram, I'll walk around a bit while you're eating. I'm still cramped from the long ride." Fonnie nodded. Brian wandered down the hall.

Keisha turned to leave when Fonnie stopped her. "Could you do me a big favor?"

The aide nodded. "Sure. What do you need?"

"To have the room to myself this afternoon. Think you could keep Lila away?"

Keisha grinned. "Will do. I'll tell her Ginger needs her advice on planning some activity. She loves to give advice. Of course, Ginger may never forgive me."

FONNIE FINISHED HER LUNCH, pushed the over-bed table aside, closed her eyes. But before she could drift into a little nap, Brian entered the room with Jock at his heels. Jock ambled over to the bed. "Missed you at lunch, gal. Had to come see for myself that you were okay."

"I'll make it. I'm a tough old broad. But I appreciate your concern."

"Everybody's upset about what happened to you. It's hard to imagine that pipsqueak Lucas as a murderer, though. I knew he was weird, but I never thought he was a maniac. Brian got me up to speed on everything. He said you suspected Lucas right from the beginning. Is that right?"

"Yes, that's right," Fonnie said, wondering if Brian mentioned that she also had three other suspects in the beginning. "But let's not talk about that now."

There was a sharp rap at the door. A volunteer glided in, her arms loaded with mail. Fonnie seldom received any U.S. postal mail anymore, just an occasional card from a member of her old Sunday School class, so she was surprised when the mail lady handed her a large manila envelope. "Looks like you hit the jackpot today. Something you ordered?"

"No. I can't imagine what it is." She looked at the address to make sure it was for her. Sure enough. That was her name.

"Who's it from, Gram?"

Fonnie studied the return address. "Harry Mullis."

"That's Hannah's son. What on earth could he be sending me?"

"Let's open it and find out."

Fonnie took her right forefinger, slid it down the sealed top. As the envelope popped open, she saw that it was crammed with pieces of newspaper.

"What could these be?"

Fonnie's curiosity was like a pot about to boil over. "Quick, Brian, dump these out. Jock, spread them out. Let's see what we have."

Brian jettisoned the contents of the envelope over the top of Fonnie's bed. Jock rescued some paper that threatened to slide to the floor. "Old newspaper clippings," Brian said. "This one's dated over fifty years ago." On top of the clippings was a note. Brian picked it up and read it out loud.

Dear Mrs. Beachum,
I remembered you asked me if Mother ever mentioned a man named Deacon. When my sisters and I were going through Mother's stuff, we found these clippings in a box. They're from her young days before she was married. I think she was in Junior College at the time. I noticed they're about a man being on trial for murder and that his nickname was Deacon. I don't know what it had to do with Mother, but since you asked, I thought you might be interested. You may keep them or toss them as you wish.
Harry Mullis

Jock grabbed a clipping and dropped down on the chair by the bed. "Oh, no," he moaned, "how could I have been so dense? Why didn't I recognize him?"

Fonnie and Brian stared at Jock. Fonnie shifted her weight so she could look over Jock's shoulder. The clipping showed a picture of a wide-eyed young man with a prominent Adam's apple. He was handsome, kindly looking. "It's Lucas Parker," Fonnie said. She leaned closer to read the article heading. "But the name here is Lucas Peaceman."

Fonnie studied the picture. "That's why Hannah said his name didn't fit. He wasn't a peaceable man."

"And that's why we couldn't find out any information about Lucas Parker," Brian said. "He didn't exist." Brian picked up another article. "It says here he killed a college student for trying to stop a cock fight. Strangled him with a piece of baling twine."

Fonnie's right hand flew up to her throat. "Omigawd." She looked over at Jock again whose face had become as pale as skim milk. "You knew him then?"

Jock slowly nodded his head. "Yes. I prosecuted him. It was one of my first cases. Open and shut. Plenty of witnesses. I asked for a life sentence and that's what he got." Jock took off his glasses and rubbed his eyes. "I should have recognized him here. How could I have forgotten that evil face? If I had identified him, Ida Mae and the others might still be alive."

Fonnie reached over and patted Jock's arm. "You couldn't have known. He assumed a different name, a different persona. And he was supposed to be in jail. There was no reason for you to remember someone from so long ago."

Brian was flipping through some of the other clippings. He handed one to Jock. "Remember him?"

Jock took the clipping and a slow smile crossed his lips. It showed a young J. C. Jowoski with a full head of hair, talking to news reporters.

"Yeah. That was me about a hundred years ago—in another life."

Fonnie took the picture, compared the young man in the photograph to the old man by her side.

"I must say you were a handsome son-of-a-gun." She hesitated, then added, "Of course, you still are."

Jock raised his eyebrows. "And you need new glasses. But thanks anyway."

Jock looked at the picture again. "I was a doggone good prosecutor though. The defense attorney argued for not guilty due to insanity, said Lucas should be sent to a mental hospital.

"The defense brought up all the shit about an abused childhood, mother died in a fire, his off-beat religious zeal. Doctors argued that he had diminished capacity. I didn't buy any of it. Sure he was crazy, but there was nothing diminished about his capacity for meanness. He was one of those sidewalk preachers, condemning everyone else to Hell while at the same time he was raising hell. He was into moonshine and cock fights and prostitution. He said his hands were God's hands. He claimed he had to kill the kid because God told him to. He was guilty of murder. And I made sure he'd spend the rest of his life in prison. Or at least I thought I had."

"But he was paroled?"

"I guess. He was probably a model prisoner. Apparently the parole board thought he was too old to be a danger to anyone. Some people think evil wanes with age, but I think it just becomes more embedded in the brain." Jock picked up another clipping. It showed a picture of the murdered boy: young, attractive, the future ahead of him. "One of the kids testified that after a cock fight, Lucas would take the injured roosters and wring their necks with his bare hands. And when this kid tried to stop him, Lucas grabbed a piece of twine, spun it around the kid's neck, and strangled him." Jock put his head in his hands. "I thought I'd stopped him. I thought I'd put him away for good. But he swore he'd get revenge on me, on the judge, on the college kids who were witnesses against him."

Fonnie caught her breath. "So it was *you* he came here to kill?"

"Must have been. Instead, he killed three other people."

Brian flipped through the rest of the clippings. "This one mentions his nickname. Says the college kids called him Deacon because he was always preaching to them. And this one says Peaceman was a high-school dropout, but that he had taken classes at the Divine Rapture Bible Institute." Brian shook his head in bewilderment. "I guess we'll never understand what battles were being fought in his head." Brian folded the clippings and placed them back in the envelope. "I'll give these to Officer Daniels. It'll make the job of tracing Lucas's background easier."

"First help me into my wheelchair. I've lain around here in bed long enough. We'll deliver these to the police, and then I want to go out on the patio, soak up a little sun."

"I'm going to pass on the patio," Jock said, "and finish reading the morning paper. I think I prefer today's bad news over yesterday's."

When the trio reached the day room, Fonnie noticed King Tut was again enthroned on Jock's favorite chair.

"Looks like Tut has taken up squatter's rights again."
She laughed.

Jock shrugged. "That's okay. He can have the chair."

Fonnie could hardly believe what she'd just heard.
Was Jock mellowing? Was he actually becoming fond
of the cats? That thought was quickly dispelled with his
next words.

"There's a spring coming loose in the cushion. I hope
it jabs him in the ass like it did me."

IT WAS A LOVELY spring afternoon. The patio caught,
enclosed, intensified the sun's warmth. The sky was so
clear there wasn't even a cloud big enough for an angel
to hide behind. The tulips, just peeking out a few days
ago, were now nearly in full bloom.

Fonnie wanted to forget Lucas and the murders, but
there were a couple more things about them she had to
discuss with Brian. "Will you call your mother and give
her an abridged account of what happened? Clean it up
the best you can. I don't want her rushing down here and
packing me up."

"Yeah, I'll call her. But are you sure you don't want
to pack? We could place you in a nice home somewhere
else. Then you wouldn't be haunted with the bad
memories here."

"Memories are strange creatures, Brian. They don't
reside in a building or a particular place. They can't be
crammed into a box or a closet or hidden under the bed.
I've learned that one has to make friends with memories—the good ones, the bad ones, the insignificant

ones. You never know when they'll show up for tea or for a bedtime visit. But if we're pleasant to them, and chat a little, then they'll soon be on their way—until the next time they decide to drop in."

"Sounds like something straight out of a pop-psychology book." Brian twisted around in his chair. "So you're saying you want to stay here?"

"Yes. This is my home now." The statement surprised Fonnie herself. But she knew it was true. This time she wasn't trying to put up a good front, wasn't telling a fib to make her family feel better. She had stepped into, or rather wheeled into, she thought wryly, the next phase of her life. And she would live it to the fullest.

"Speaking of home," Brian started, cleared his throat. "Speaking of your home, that is, your house...."

Fonnie interrupted another throat clearing. "I think you're trying to tell me something. So out with it."

"Would you mind putting off selling it for a few months? You see, I was talking to some of the policemen while you were eating lunch. And I told them I wanted to go into law enforcement and they said there were several openings here and that it was an excellent force and a great place to work. And so, I thought after I graduated, I'd move here, get a job, and buy your house."

Fonnie slapped the arm of her wheelchair with her right hand, her grin puffed her cheeks out as if she had mumps, and she emitted an uncharacteristic giggle. "Oh, my, that's marvelous news."

"I figured it'd be a whole lot easier than moving all my toys you saved."

"And my unicorn collection. I've been agonizing over what to do with my unicorns. Can I just leave them with you?"

"I won't disturb them a bit. And I'll have a ramp built from the carport to the back door so you can come visit me and them anytime you wish."

Fonnie's eyes glistened at the thought.

TWENTY-TWO

LIEUTENANT MCELROY came out to the patio just as Brian was leaving. Fonnie introduced them. "Brian is on spring break and is anxious to get back to the beach."

"I don't blame him. I wouldn't mind a little break myself."

"Maybe you can get one," Brian said, "now that you've solved this case."

The detective shook his head. "I didn't solve this case. The credit for that goes to your grandmother." He slid a yard chair up closer to Fonnie. "My congratulations and my apology."

"Apologies? For what?"

"For not believing you when you were trying to tell me of the other suspicious deaths. And for not letting you tell me about your suspects. If I had, your close call with death might have been avoided."

"Apology accepted. On one condition."

"And that is?"

"The next time an old duffer tries to tell you something, don't assume that the mind is shriveled up just because the body is."

"Believe me. I won't make that mistake again." He stretched out his hand. "Friends?"

"Friends," Fonnie said, and shook his hand. "But I was wondering about one other thing."

"And that would be?"

"Something I've been worried about. Will you have to exhume the bodies of Lit and Hannah to prove how they really died?"

The detective shook his head. "No. I've discussed it with my chief, and we both think that would be unnecessary, as well as causing emotional trauma to the families. We'll have to tell the families, however, about Mr. Peaceman's confession to you, but I think that will be the end of it. I don't see how they could place any blame on the nursing home."

"Good. Hannah and Lit deserve to rest in peace. And the rest of us need to move on."

THAT EVENING Fonnie was glad to be back in the dining room again. The Four Musketeers waved at her from their corner table. Others smiled and called out greetings. Maggie came in from the kitchen and gave her a hug. And to think only a week ago, Fonnie thought, she'd been afraid she wouldn't have any friends here.

The supper menu read *spaghetti and Texas toast*. Fonnie sniffed appreciatively of tomato paste and garlic. She smiled at Oliver as he came in. She motioned him to come sit with her. He came over to her table, but his gaze went to another table. "If it's all the same with you,

I'll sit with Tillie. She needs someone to remind her to eat." He looked down at his feet and mumbled, "Now that Lucas is gone."

"Of course. You go right ahead."

Jock and Calvin came in together and joined her. The conversation centered around the food, the weather, the Spring Fling that Ginger was planning. They carefully avoided any mention of the morning's events. Fonnie was glad. She knew that in days to come something would be said about Lucas, about Hannah and Lit, about their near escape from a devastating fire, and when that time came, she would handle it. But for now she needed the respite.

Calvin finished his meal first. "Guess I'll go to the computer room and check on my stocks."

Calvin's estrangement from his son bothered Fonnie, and she suddenly decided to try to do something about it. "Why don't you e-mail your son while you're there?"

The suggestion took Calvin by surprise. After a few moments he replied, "I don't know his address."

"The social worker has it in your admitting file."

Both Calvin and Jock stared at Fonnie. Jock blurted out, "And how would you know that, Miss Nosy?"

Uh-oh, Fonnie thought. *I've tripped myself up. I can't let them know I peeked at the files. I'm not about to confess to unlawful entry—especially since my grandson is going to be a cop.* She did some quick thinking and came up with a plausible explanation.

"When I was admitted, Amy had to give them her

e-mail address along with her home address and two telephone numbers where she could be reached. So, I assume, they have the same information on your son." Fonnie smiled at her own cleverness. "The social worker is still here. You could ask her to look."

Calvin bobbed his head. "Yes. I could do that. Ken might be interested in how my stocks are doing."

Fonnie watched Calvin skim his walker down the hall, head held high, shoulders back.

Jock crunched his last bite of Texas toast, wiped his mouth with the back of his hand. "Think you're pretty smart, don't you?"

"Not really. You see there's one puzzle which I can't solve."

"Maybe I can help. What's the problem?"

Fonnie took a long sip of her iced tea, swirled the piece of lemon around, put on a serious face. "That newspaper clipping gave your initials as J.C. And I'm very curious to find out what J. C. Jowoski's real name is."

Jock exploded in laughter. The remaining diners gawked over to their table. Fonnie waited patiently. "It's a secret I've told to only my best friends," he said.

"Then I think I qualify."

"Indeed you do." He lowered his voice and whispered across the table. "But you must promise it won't go any further."

"I promise."

"My real name is Julius Caesar. You see, my mother

was a Romo-phile. She adored all the emperors, and she had rather high hopes for me. She thought I would become a leader among men."

"Oh, you have," Fonnie said. "You've just won the award for being the biggest liar in the country. And I guess I'll have to keep snooping until I find out the truth."

"That's right," Jock said. "I figure you need a little something to keep your brain cells working."

FONNIE HAD A HARD TIME forcing herself out of bed in the morning. It was Wednesday and she was scheduled for her therapy session. She hadn't realized before just how difficult it would be to go back to the physical therapy room. She reasoned with herself that the whirl-pool wouldn't be on, and that Andy would be there, but still it would be hard. She dawdled in the bathroom until Carlotta scolded her. "You won't have time to eat breakfast before therapy if you don't hurry."

She wanted to say that her stomach wasn't up to breakfast this morning, but she allowed herself to be dressed and pushed out the door. When she came out of the bathroom, she was met with Lila's fierce eyes. "I'm sorry," Fonnie said. "It took me a little longer than usual this morning. The bathroom is all yours now."

"That's all right," her roommate said.

Fonnie thought it looked as if the ends of Lila's thin mouth were curved slightly upward. Could it be the beginning of a smile? Or was it just a trick of the over-bed light?

"You see, there's no hurry now," Lila said. "I've already wet my bed."

AFTER BREAKFAST, Fonnie made a detour back to the day room to find Sheba. Maybe the trip to PT would be easier if she had her friend with her. Sheba had recovered from her near death experience, and was busy making her ankle massage rounds. Fonnie wheeled up to her just as the cat finished with Oliver and headed toward the TV viewers. Fonnie patted her lap and invited Sheba to jump into it. "Want to go for a ride, Sheba?"

Sheba studied the wheelchair, its occupant, and the direction it was headed. Apparently the cat decided she didn't need another bath. She turned her head and flounced over to Gwendolyn. Fonnie sighed and headed toward hall D.

Andy and his assistant, Elga, were waiting for her, just as they'd been on Monday. Could that have been only two days ago? It seemed a lifetime ago. Of course, the therapists knew all about yesterday, but they made no reference to it. Andy was all business. Fonnie could tell he wanted to get started. He didn't even ask her how she was, or drawl her name out to three syllables. "We'll work on the walking bars again."

She was in position, belt around her waist, Andy by her side, Elga behind her with the wheelchair, when Jock entered the room. He walked between the bars, came up close to her, and bowed slightly. He gave her a dazzling smile. "May I have this dance?"

Andy grabbed Jock's arm. "You can't come in here like this."

Fonnie smiled at her friend. She turned to Andy. "It's all right."

Jock came closer, put his left arm around her waist, clutched the belt, and picked up her right hand. He turned to Andy. "Would you place her left hand on my shoulder?"

Andy hesitated. Fonnie gave him a go-ahead look. Andy took her left hand off the rail, placed it on Jock's shoulder, wrapped her fingers around the red suspender.

Jock started humming an unrecognizable tune. "Now let me lead," he said to his partner. Andy and Elga gawked at the couple. The therapists made no attempt to interfere, but neither did they back away. Jock swayed and rocked and wobbled and teetered. He even attempted a dip, a Barney Fife special. It didn't matter that their feet barely moved at all. They were dancing.

Fonnie was transported to another world, another era. She was young. She was beautiful. She had on a low-cut pink nylon dress with a full skirt that swirled out when she spun around. She had her life ahead of her. It was going to be a wonderful life.

The song ended. Jock bowed again, placed her right hand back on the bar. "Thank you for the dance," he said. Andy repositioned her left hand, took hold of the belt, and Jock stepped away.

Fonnie nodded, whispered, "And thank you."